Dressed to Kill

to

Kill

AN ANTIQUE HUNTERS MYSTERY

5

VICKI VASS

Dedicated to Rachel Contraldes for sharing her love of collecting wax seals and to Luna and Reina for inspiring the story.

The Bee's Knees, Spoon Sisters Blog

D*EAR FRIENDS,*
    Where to start? So many changes over the past few months, I apologize for not posting more frequently. Anne and I have taken over stewardship of the Bee's Knees farm in Hampshire. I have walked every inch of this forty-acre farm, and on each walk I have discovered new vistas of wildflowers. Spring beauties, pink and fragrant; beechdrops greet me with their cream and purple arms; wild ginger; green dragon; daffodils; and violets. Some evenings I find myself transported into an ancient world amongst the oak, ash, and thorn. The original caretaker, a direct descendant of the Druids, planted a hidden circle of these old world trees believing that they held great power. I feel that power as their canopy closes over me, engulfing me in their magic. Each week I walk the well-worn path to the back ten acres to harvest the most delicious organic honey you'll ever taste.

    The heart of the farm is the 19th century farmhouse, which we recently painted white. The wraparound porch gives a welcoming smile to those who visit. The Bee's Knees Café is nestled at the back of the house in the old sunroom. Be sure to stop in for a true farm-to-table, literally farm-to-table, breakfast, lunch, and Sunday dinner. We plan to offer brunch soon. All the chickens are free range and the vegetables are fresh from our gardens. As many of you know from earlier blogs, I love gardening so managing this farm has been a dream come true.

    While I've focused on the fields, Anne has spent hours converting the barn into an antique store, stocking it with items that are too large for our Glen Ellyn store, Great-Aunt Sybil's Attic. She continues to maintain our wish list for you, our fans, and to search for fabulous finds to stock both stores.

For those of you new to the blog, my twenty-year-old niece Ingrid, from Germany, is still staying with me. Now a sophomore at Columbia College, she is majoring in journalism and recently accompanied me on a tour of a steel mill in Gary, Indiana. When not in school, she helps out at both the antique store and at the Bee's Knees Café. After our soft launch, the café became so popular we had to hire a local chef. Many of his recipes stem from my collection.

To celebrate our opening, we are hosting today's auction to benefit the Greater Chicago Family Fund. We were inspired after meeting Dakota, 9, and her mother, Caroline, at a block sale event. Not only have they become permanent employees at our store, they've also become great friends. Anne has taken a special interest in Dakota, mentoring her on antiques and collectibles.

Now about the dress, so many of you have written to us about Anne's find at the Treasure House, a Civil War era-ball gown. I've posted pictures of the blue silk and black beaded dress below. Since finding it, Anne has been on its trail, trying to discover its history. She believes it to be an original Elizabeth Keckley gown. Miss Keckley was Mary Todd Lincoln's dressmaker. Until she is better able to authenticate it, Anne feels she cannot in good conscience include it in today's auction. If it is an original Keckley dress, it might be priceless. However, Anne has agreed to put it on display. You will find it in the front hallway of the farmhouse, but she does ask that you refrain from touching it.

We do have many other items up for auction including a very rare Davidoff malachite-and-gold vase from Imperial Russia, and my favorite, a pair of 18-karat flowered earrings with natural blue sapphires repurposed from an Art Deco bracelet.

After our recent adventures, our lives have changed so greatly. Anne has taken her new role as an amateur sleuth quite seriously, picturing herself as a modern day Nancy Drew. Like Nancy, trouble seems to find us. The world of antique hunting can be perilous, but the reward is worth the risk.

I have found refuge in the peaceful beauty of this place. It calms my heart and rejuvenates my spirit. It makes me appreciate the gift that each day brings and the importance of sharing that gift with family. When I first started this blog, I wrote with a jour-

nalistic eye, telling my story from a distance, but I can no longer keep that distance, because you, my dear friends, have become our family. From this entry on, I take you with me, whatever peril may come.

Hope to see you at the auction. For now, dear friends, too-dooloo.

CC closed her laptop, glancing out the second floor window. She could see the preparations were well underway. Her best friend and fellow antique hunter, Anne, was darting from place to place, moving her arms frantically, only stopping to inspect items. Wait. CC peered more closely out the window. She grabbed her bird watching binoculars. Tags labeled "NFS" in large letters with black permanent marker were streaming out of Anne's hands. CC sighed. This would not do. She ran outside, crossed the lawn, and entered the tent. Then she followed in Anne's path, removing the "not for sale" tags from item after item and rearranging the auction collection to its best advantage. She would have to keep a watchful eye on her friend today.

Standing back, she surveyed the exhibit area. "Done," she exclaimed, clapping her hands together. Wooden benches were lined in neatly placed rows facing an antique oak lectern Anne had dug out of one of her numerous storage lockers. Anne had a penchant for collecting that was always slightly bigger than her space. The lectern had been rescued from a soon-to-be demolished church on Chicago's South Side. Several long tables to the side of the lectern held an eclectic collection of antique and vintage items, ranging from textiles to toys to crystal to music boxes. While many of these items had been sprung from Anne's inventory, others had been donated for the day. CC had spent the past weeks collecting and cataloging donations for the sale. Each piece had been scrubbed, polished until it gleamed for its moment on the block. "Anne, stop," CC said, running up to the front when she saw Anne undoing her handiwork. "What's going on? I had everything organized according to its number in the catalog."

"I was double checking that everything was numbered correctly," Anne said, cradling a Staffordshire bone china springer spaniel dog. Although not particularly a dog lover herself, she had a weakness for porcelain dogs, and this one would fit perfectly in her personal collection.

"Anne, put that down. We decided to include it in the auction," CC said, reaching for the china figure.

Anne slowly put the dog back on the table, her fingers lingering over it as if to snatch it back up. Perhaps she could stick it in the pocket of her pants, THE PANTS, the flowered capris she had won, the ones that had once belonged to B movie star Kim Povak. With the crowd they were expecting, CC would never notice. She couldn't recall every piece that they had selected for the auction. Though Anne definitely could. Over the past few weeks, while CC had photographed and cataloged the items for the auction, Anne had made painstaking notes beside each one. Her notes included purchase date, price paid, and any known provenance. She pulled her hand back from the dog. Today was not the day to remove it for her personal collection. Today was a very important day for the Antique Hunters. Today they had invited their growing list of fans and followers to a charity auction, and the reputation of their antique store depended on a stellar day.

A young girl walked up to her, bearing a silver tray filled with glasses of fresh lemonade. "Miss Anne, is this ok?"

"Oh, dear, yes." Anne smiled at the young girl, little Dakota, the girl she had been mentoring over the past year. The proceeds from today's auction were going to an organization that helped families like Dakota's who were struggling to keep food on the table. Seeing Dakota reminded Anne that she could and should part with her treasures.

"Miss CC wants me to stand by the gate," Dakota said.

"You look wonderful," Anne said. Dakota was wearing an apple green dress that had once belonged to Anne's cousin's young daughter. She watched Dakota walk to the bottom of the long driveway before heading back toward the old farmhouse.

"Anne, where's the dress? People have been asking to see it." CC's voice came up from behind her. "You know the Keckley one? I thought we had agreed to put it on display."

Shoving her hands in her pant pockets, Anne turned around. She avoided CC's penetrating gaze as well as the question about the dress. Anne was having second thoughts about putting it on display for all to see. What if it was ruined?

"Anne, where is it?" CC stared down her friend, reminding herself to keep her patience. Anne struggled continuously with sharing and parting with her purchases. Time was of the essence as CC could see the cars streaming in, and the dress was to be the showstopper. Nick, CC's boyfriend, and some of his Glen Ellyn firefighters were already directing drivers toward the makeshift parking lot in the south field.

"It's not for sale. It's not in the auction catalog," Anne said.

"After I blogged about it, a lot of people said they wanted to see it. I told them it would be on display today."

"I. . .I. . . wanted to do some additional research on it," Anne said, picturing the dress in its hiding place hanging in her bathroom. "I didn't feel right displaying the dress without authenticating it. I did learn that it was donated from the Sharon Prima estate, so I contacted the company handling the estate sale. Sharon had no surviving relatives. She had a small house in Glen Ellyn and nothing worth much of value except for the dress."

"I can start from there. I'll do some research on Sharon Prima. I have to go help Nick," CC said before rushing to help direct traffic down the long gravel driveway.

Anne stared after her friend. She was torn. She believed because she believed this dress dated back to the Civil War. Its handsewn label read "Isobel Grant" and then "Elizabeth Keckley". Anne had found the dress in an old trunk that had been donated to the resale shop where she volunteered. She had recognized Keckley's name at once, but she couldn't find any reference to a woman named Isobel, even one related to the famous Ulysses S. She must research the gown to find out its history. There was no way she was going to bring it out at this sale, not until she knew exactly what it was. She needed more information. It wouldn't be fair to the eventual buyer or to her. She sank down on one of the benches and tapped her foot impatiently. Her research would have to wait until after this auction. CC would have to wait. There was no time.

Gazing around the space, she marveled at the scene before her. CC had outdone herself organizing everything from the big tent that shaded the auction bidders to the podium with the line of items. The auction catalog was both in print and online. Dakota stood at the front gate, greeting arrivals with a cheery smile and fresh lemonade. Seated at a front table was the beautiful young Ingrid, assigning numbers and paddles to those wanting to bid. Several groups gathered on the wooden front porch of the old farmhouse, which had been adorned with daffodils and tulips. English ivy wrapped around its tall columns. Spring had burst onto the farm in the far western reaches of Chicago. The place was turning into the perfect accompaniment to their growing empire—the blog which constantly brought them new fans, their antique store Great-Aunt Sybil's Attic, and now this farmhouse café, honey farm, and barn sale. Perhaps she could leave a permanent collection of primitive antiques here to entice shoppers.

"No," she screamed, turning the heads of several onlookers as she caught a glimpse of periwinkle blue sliding into a parking spot near the front of the gate. "No," she repeated. No, not today. It couldn't be.

"Anne, what's wrong?" CC ran over to her.

Anne pointed. "Buttersworth," she roared. A small starling startled by the eruption fell from its perch in the rafters, righting itself before hitting the ground and flying to safety. That car could only mean one thing. The arrival of her long-time antique hunting nemesis, Betsy Buttersworth. No relation to the syrup but ever a sticky problem. It could wreck her day. She didn't want to share this, the Antique Hunters first auction at the Bee's Knees, with Buttersworth. For a brief period, they had celebrated a truce but the amnesty had subsided in light of shopping misadventures. Prizes won, prizes lost. Anne had stopped her tally but only knew she couldn't lose this round. Bid, she would. She swiped up a paddle with a number written in black permanent marker, scribbled her name on Ingrid's check-in sheet, and then stomped to the front row. She would win this round.

"Anne, calm down." CC followed her to the seat. "You're not supposed to bid. We're hosting. It doesn't look right."

"Hillstrom," a cultured voice said from across the aisle.

"Buttersworth." Anne nodded in return, capturing the seat on the aisle directly across from Betsy Buttersworth. The perfectly coiffed and polished Buttersworth, always dressing past the nines into the tens. Her fortune made the old-fashioned way, wealthy ex-husbands.

The early morning sun filtered through the billowing white tent, illuminating the makeshift podium. CC walked up, tapped it with a gavel. "Thank you everyone for coming to today's auction to benefit the Greater Chicago Family Rescue. All proceeds will be donated to help with their fine work providing assistance to families in need."

Anne glanced sideways at Buttersworth's five-carat alexandrite ring, glistening brilliantly in the sunlight. She thought about how many homes that could provide. Jimmy Choo heels. Surely four months' rent. What about her periwinkle blue silk Vince tunic? A half year of utility bills. Anne's thoughts returned to the auction as CC waved her to the stage.

Anne grabbed the first item, a copper fire extinguisher, from its table and dragged it to the front. She placed it on the small display cabinet next to the podium.

"First item up for bid," the auctioneer began. "An early twentieth century fire extinguisher taken from the Tribune Tower."

Anne had wanted to keep the extinguisher, but her former next-door neighbor Grandma Jan wouldn't sell it to her even after Anne said she would give the money to charity. Grandma Jan had issues with Anne's over-collecting as she referred to it. "We'll start the bidding at fifty dollars," the auctioneer continued.

Before he could finish his sentence, Betsy raised her paddle. He nodded, acknowledging her. As Anne raised her paddle, CC pulled her arm down. Anne clutched the paddle in her lap, counting silently to ten in her head. The auction continued. Each item found a good home, orphaned artifact matched with a new loving family.

"I'm going to check on the kitchen," CC said to Anne before leaving. Anne continued to watch the auction. Item after item flew by, the bidding fast and furious. It left a bittersweet taste in her mouth. Until the *piece de resistance* came up. She couldn't contain herself anymore. It was a set of Weathersby china, not vintage, not even old, but lovely just the same. She had coveted this set. It had taken her years to find it. And find it she did, hidden in the dusty basement of a suburban house. Waiting for her. It pained her to part with it. She wouldn't part, not today.

Buttersworth quickly opened the bidding. Anne followed. Their paddles flew up and down until Anne lost track of who was the victor. "Sold," she heard the auctioneer say as the hammer went down. "Two thousand dollars. Number 54." There was silence and then Anne glanced at the paddle resting in her lap. She had won. Wait, she had won. She had bested Buttersworth. "How much?" she asked. It dawned on her that she didn't have the funds. She would have to figure something out.

When the last lot had been sold, Anne wandered to the front table where Ingrid was collecting the payments. Anne ran her finger along the column that read Buttersworth and continued on to the next page. She shook her head.

"What about the dress?" A voice called out from behind her.

Anne turned to see an elegant woman classically garbed in a St. John suit with a matching Hermes silk scarf. What a smartly dressed woman, she thought. "Excuse me?"

"The dress," the woman repeated a soft drawl to her voice. "I came for the dress. You are Miss Hillstrom, right?"

Anne's heart skipped a beat. "Yes, of course. How did you know?"

"I recognized you from the blog. What about the dress?"

"Oh, yes, there's a little bit of confusion. We weren't able to display it today."

"May I see it?" The woman asked.

"Oh, it's not here. I left it back at our store." Anne turned away to talk to Ingrid, who now stood holding a tray of wine glasses filled with a lovely cabernet.

The woman grabbed Anne by the arm and twirled her back around. As she did, she bumped the tray, spilling wine on the woman's dress.

"I'm so sorry. What a beautiful dress. Ingrid, run and get some club soda," Anne said, handing her a napkin.

The woman attempted to sop up the wine. Anne tried to help, but the woman waved her off. "It's ok. It's ok, really." She glanced at Anne again. "I'm sorry, Miss Hillstrom, but it's very important that I see the dress."

CC came up to them, overhearing the conversation. "What's going on?"

"This woman—I'm sorry, I didn't get your name?"

"Lindsey Kelly."

"Miss Kelly came about the dress. I was explaining to her that it was not on display today."

CC shook Miss Kelly's hand. "I'm so sorry for the inconvenience. There was an issue with authenticating the dress. It will be available at the auction next month."

"I drove all the way from Springfield just to see that dress. I saw your blog and was intrigued by your description and the photos."

"We're very sorry."

Lindsey glanced at her Fendi watch.

Anne thought that's a year's worth of groceries.

"I have a conference call I have to take. Can I stop by your store and see it?" Lindsey asked.

"I'm sorry, but we'll be cleaning up here and closing the café. The store is closed today," Anne said.

CC interrupted. "Again, I'm sorry you came all this way. How about we bring the dress to you? Where are you staying?"

"That would be wonderful. I'm staying at the Loew's in Rosemont. I'm driving back in the morning."

"We'd be happy to bring the dress to you later tonight."

Lindsey reached inside her Hermes alligator bag. "Alligator," Anne whispered, unable to imagine how many homeless families that purse would feed.

Handing CC a business card, Lindsey walked away, leaving an air of opulence behind. Anne wafted in its scent. Her current financial situation held a less pleasant odor.

When CC entered the Bee's Knee Café was buzzing with patrons. Ingrid and Dakota's mother, Caroline, were taking orders. In the kitchen, Nick stirred a mushroom sauce which stirred emotions in CC. Reaching around Nick, she lifted the lid on a pan to uncover a roasted chicken. "That's not Henrietta, is it?" CC whispered.

"No, that's Whole Foods, I didn't have the heart," Nick whispered.

"So much for farm to table." CC wrapped her arms around Nick's waist, taking in the smell of firehouse smoke and herbed chicken. She glanced over her shoulder and saw the copper fire extinguisher. "What's that doing here? Nick peered over his shoulder. "Oh, your friend, Betsy. She gave it to me for the bar."

"She gave it to you. Why'd she give it to you?"

Nick shrugged.

"Oh," CC said. She grabbed an apron and stirred the mashed potatoes. "Mmm." She added a pinch of garlic followed by another of her very special ingredient, ghost pepper powder.

Nick gave her a look.

"Just a pinch, Nick, just a pinch. It makes everything better."

Nick smiled.

Time flew by as they served their customers. Finally, Anne closed the door behind the last guest, locking it with a click. Ingrid sat at a table counting her tips. She pulled out a twenty-dollar bill and handed it to Dakota. "You did a great job helping today, Dakota."

The girl smiled and looked at her mother for approval, who gave it.

"Anne, let's go," CC said, coming out of the kitchen, wiping her hands on a towel.

"I'm ready to go home," Anne agreed.

"No, we're going to pick up the dress and stop by the hotel."

CC gave Nick a kiss. She and Anne climbed into CC's 1968 VW bus.

"Why do we have to bring her the dress?" Anne asked. "I don't even know if it is real or not. We don't know who she is."

CC turned an eye toward Anne. "She came a long way for that dress we advertised. The least we can do is let her take a look at it."

"I don't know. I didn't get a good feeling from her," Anne replied.

"Why don't you text her and tell her we'll be there about ten? I got her card somewhere in here." CC took her hand off the wheel and shoved a hand into the pocket of her overalls. She swerved toward the shoulder, sending gravel flying into the windshield.

"CC!"

"I know, I know." She righted the car. "Here it is." She handed the crumpled card to Anne.

Anne studied the card for a moment. "Did you look at this?"

"No, I've been too busy. I shoved it in my pocket."

"It says she's the assistant curator at the Lincoln Presidential Library and Museum in Springfield." Anne's eyes lit up. She had never visited the museum and its collection of Mary Todd Lincoln dresses. If Lindsey had driven all the way for the dress, Anne's dress, it could be authentic.

"I had no idea," CC said.

"We should get the dress right now," Anne said, texting a quick message saying, "We're on our way."

CC smiled.

A short while later, CC pulled up in front of the store in downtown Glen Ellyn.

"I'll be right out." Anne jumped out of the car, fumbling with the keys. Anne had no idea of what was waiting behind the door. When she opened it, her white Persian Sassy and her kitten, Sybil, lunged at her, purring and meandering around her legs. "I know. I know. I'm a bit late. A quick dinner. I must run. You have no idea who I'm meeting with tonight." Sassy and Sybil were neither comforted nor amused by Anne's words. They held to their purpose, almost dragging her through the showroom of antiques to the backroom kitchenette. The Persians leapt to the shelf over the small '50s red and white chrome kitchen table. The two furry gargoyles watched carefully, waiting for the sound to summon them. Anne pressed the lid of the can opener, releasing the scent of the organic ahi tuna. A special treat Anne brought out when she felt especially guilty leaving her sweet ones alone for too long. The second the can opened, both cats leapt to the table. Anne doled out the special treat. "You two enjoy. I'm going to run upstairs and grab the dress."

Anne had forgotten to tell CC she was keeping it in her apartment above the store and occasionally wearing it at night as she read Civil War stories—including *Little Women, Gone with the Wind* and *North and South*—by the hearth. Her small attic apartment was cozy, decorated with all the things Anne loved—her favorite pink velvet chaise, her mahogany drum table, her Tiffanyesque lamp. Normally at this time of the day she would sit by the fire with her feet up, enjoying a cup of tea and a good book. Not tonight. She walked past all that and into her small bedroom to the small bathroom.

The dress was exactly where she had left it, hanging on a silk hanger on the shower rod. She marveled at the hundreds of tiny black beads and the embroidery the neck and bodice of the dress. It was a work of art. She hated to part with it. She lifted it up and carefully folded it into a garment bag. Lindsey hadn't said she wanted the gown, only that she wanted to see it. Plus she worked at the Lincoln Museum. Perhaps she would give Anne an open invitation to visit. Anne would drop everything for a behind the scenes tour.

Balancing the dress carefully over her arm, she went outside to CC's bus. "What took you so long?" CC asked as Anne got in the car.

"Sorry, I had to feed the cats." Anne folded the bag over her lap. CC drove the short distance from their store to the hotel in Rosemont, minutes from O'Hare Airport and just mere steps to the Premium Outlet mall. Anne stared longingly at the flashing yellow sign by the outlet mall, advertising sales at Nordstrom Rack, Off Fifth, Burberry and Prada.

"Not tonight," CC said as if reading her mind.

Anne glanced at the time on her iPhone. It was after nine, and all the stores were closed. Her shopping trip would have to wait for another day and would best be done alone. CC pulled into the outlet mall parking lot. "What are we doing here?"

"We can walk to the hotel from here," CC said as she pulled into a parking space on the first floor.

"Why?" Anne stared out at the football field length separating them from the hotel's back entrance.

"The hotel charges for parking. This lot is free," CC said, making sure the bus was locked before they began the trek across the parking lot.

Anne trudged along the blacktop behind CC, lifting her cargo up so as to avoid any dragging it in the damp spots on the pavement. The lights gave an eerie glow accompanied by the neon eyes from the restaurants and hotels dotting the street. They could hear the nearby traffic noise from the Tri-State Tollway and

River Road; however, the parking lot was deserted.

Entering the hotel, they strolled to the bank of elevators. Anne pressed the button for the ninth floor. Anne cradled the dress. The doors slid open and they stepped off. "She's in Room 914," Anne said, glancing at her text message.

They walked down the narrow hallway, past the closed doors, reading the brass tags next to the doors. As they approached Room 914, a sliver of light came out from the side, the door was slightly ajar. "She must have opened for us," CC said, knocking. There was no answer.

"Maybe she left," Anne said.

"Don't be silly." CC pushed the door open and stepped into the corner suite, Anne on her heels. Anne clutched the back of CC's jacket, but CC waved her off. "Really, Anne," CC said, before turning back into the room and calling out, "Miss Kelly." There was no answer.

Anne glanced around the room, an example of elegant contemporary furnishings. On the table sat an open can of Diet Coke. Across from it the 42-inch plasma was tuned to the local news. A woman's pair of black pumps lay across the floor. Anne recognized them as the ones Lindsey had been wearing earlier.

"Miss Kelly. Lindsey," CC called out again.

Anne heard a small cry, no more than a whimper. She stepped into the small kitchenette. She heard it again. "Anne, what are you doing?"

"I heard a noise." Anne flipped a switch. Two black cats stared up at Anne. "CC."

CC came over, carrying two cat carrier cases. "I found these."

"I found these," Anne replied, picking up the cats, both scared and purring. Anne read the tags on their collars, "Luna and Reina." They also wore ESA tags.

CC examined their Emotional Support Animal tags. She had a similar one for Bandit, her Australian shepherd, except Bandit was an AESA, an Animal Emotional Support Animal. Bandit comforted emotional support animals, who were stressed by their stressed owners. "They're both emotional support animals. Lindsey must travel with them."

"Don't tell Sassy." Anne smiled.

From around her friend's shoulder, Anne glimpsed through the living area into the bedroom. Perhaps Lindsay was there. Walking to the bedroom, she passed the closet and paused to admire the St. John suit and matching Hermes scarf that Lindsey wore to the auction. She touched the silk of the scarf. Next to it a Diane von Furstenberg purple wrap dress had a vintage Hermes scarf dotted with purple wrapped around its neck.

The bed called to Anne with its inviting array of fluffy pillows. She didn't realize how tired she was from the day's activities until she saw the down pillow top mattress. Maybe she could rest for a minute while they waited for Lindsey, wherever she may be. She sat on the edge of the bed; it was softer than she had imagined. She lay back, cuddling up to the pillow. Reaching over, she pulled the comforter over her feet; the walk through the parking lot had chilled her. She gave in and pulled it up around her, snuggling into the down cocoon closing her eyes. Opening one eye, she saw a pair of kitten-heeled slippers sticking out from the edge of the comforter hanging over the bed. She thought of the Wicked Witch from the *Wizard of Oz*. Anne flipped over, lifting up the comforter. The slippers weren't empty. Lindsey was lying staring up at Anne. She was wearing a beautiful Halston silver sequined dress. Her neck swollen three times normal size, her body covered in hives.

Anne screamed, then gasped out, "CC, get in here."

CC ran into the room. She knelt, checked Lindsey's pulse, then looked up at Anne, shaking her head. "She's had some kind of allergic reaction. She's gone." CC dialed 911.

After the police left, CC and Anne walked through the quiet parking lot back to the VW bus, each with a cat carrier. Neither had wanted to leave the cats behind. Anne still clutched the dress bag, clinging to it more tightly now after their ordeal. This wasn't the first dead body she had found. They, the dead bodies, seemed to find her, and she never got used to their visits. And she hadn't even had the benefit of calling her on-again, off-again boyfriend, Chicago Police Detective, the very tall and very British, Nigel Towers. He would have known what to do. He would have had the right words to calm her heart. Nigel was off somewhere after leaving her with a few words. She shivered in the late night air.

It was pitch black, the parking lot lights turned off for the night. Anne could still make out the sounds of trucks speeding along the Tri-State Tollway and the hiss of planes landing and taking off from nearby O'Hare. "The EMT said she had an allergic reaction," she said.

CC didn't answer.

"What do we do next?" Anne asked.

"For tonight, we go home. We get some rest. There's nothing we can do." CC unlocked the doors of the VW bus.

Anne settled down in the passenger seat, taking comfort from the alerts for items on her watch list at several auction sites. She had found a new favorite and was watching a French Art Deco Hanging Lantern. It might be a little large for her cozy apartment, but she could make it work. She gave CC a hug as they pulled in front of Great-Aunt Sybil's Attic. "I'll be over first thing in the morning."

"I know. I know, you will."

"Do you want me to bring bagels?"

"I can make crepes."

"The ones I like?"

"Yes, the ones you like."

Anne hugged her again and hurried out the car doors, grabbing the dress and the cat carriers. As she unlocked her door, she ignored the two ghosts in the front window. They both leapt from their perch as she opened the door. "Sassy, Sybil, this is Luna and Reina. Let's make our guests welcome," Anne said, setting down the carriers.

Sassy circled the intruders, emitting a low growl. Sybil jumped on top of Luna's crate and peeked her head upside down. "Now ladies, let's show some hospitality, shall we?"

Both cats stepped back and stood patiently. Anne opened the crates. "Come here Luna, Reina. It's ok. You're safe. Everything's ok."

Both cats huddled in the back of their crates, not moving. Anne ran up to the kitchenette, came back with an open can of tuna. Sassy and Sybil purred and rubbed along Anne's legs.

"This is for our guests," Anne scolded. She placed the can in front of the crates. Both cats came out slowly, sniffing the air, touching one paw on the wooden floor. Sassy paced back and forth, growling. Sybil watched in amazement. After a short while Luna and Reina nibbled the tuna fish, Anne stroking their fur. Sybil and Sassy leapt back into the front window, watching in disgust, seemingly whispering or plotting with each other. Anne headed up the stairs.

"It's been quite a night. Let's make some tea and a fire, and I'll tell you all about it." All four cats meandered through her legs as she climbed up the stairs. She carefully placed the dress bag on the coat hook by the front door. The hundred-year-old oak floors creaked under her feet. A comforting sound, a familiar sound. She moved several boxes out of her way so she could walk into her kitchenette. The boxes contained the contents from a recent estate sale; she had bought them sight unseen. "I know, I know, guys, I can hear CC now. Half of these things will be going downstairs, the rest will be going on eBay."

Sassy and her minion leapt up to the kitchen table and watched Anne prepare the tea. "Chamomile," she said over her shoulder. As the kettle boiled, Anne checked the pantry. She brought out the last Tupperware container full of shortbread cookies. She loaded up the fireplace with logs and applewood kindling she had salvaged from CC's backyard. She loved the smell of applewood in the fireplace. She sunk down into the red leather wingback chair in front of the fire. She had made this attic her home. She reached into her large orange Prada bag and retrieved Lindsey's business card. She flipped it between her fingers. The etched gold lettering spoke highly of the woman who carried it. "Who are you, Lindsey?" Anne asked out loud. Sybil's response was a soft meow as she landed on Anne's lap.

Anne glanced over at the leather top drum table and the 8 x 10 of Nigel in his Chicago police blues. His bony shoulders holding up his jacket like a coat hanger, his silly grin, his attempt at a pencil thin moustache, his beautiful sparkling eyes and loving smile. It had been nearly three months since he had said goodbye on her doorstep, and not a word since. The teakettle whistled. Anne carefully reached into her china cabinet and pulled out a Meissen teacup. This occasion called for the best cup in the house, and the eighteenth-century bone china teacup was that cup.

Anne wrapped a kitchen towel around the handle of the tea-kettle and turned off the burner. "Aunt Sybil," she said. The tea-kettle was Aunt Sybil's orphaned artifact, once owned by Sir Arthur Conan Doyle. It was left to Anne with the promise that she would carry on its tradition. Anne filled her teacup. When there was a problem to be solved, a mystery to unravel, this was the teakettle. This was the teakettle Aunt Sybil used to play tea party with Anne and her cousin, Suzanne, when they were little. This was the teakettle in which Aunt Sybil brewed their special teas and read to them the *Hounds of the Baskerville*. This was the tea-kettle that Anne would pour from tonight as she pondered what had happened to Lindsey.

She sat in front of the fire, sipping her tea, reaching down to a pile of books. The first was a fictional account of Mary Todd Lincoln and her relationship with her dressmaker. "It's going to be a long night," she said to the cats as though they understood. Sybil and Sassy jumped onto the ottoman and lay across Anne's feet. Their warmth comforted her. She drifted off, dreaming she was wearing her ball gown and twirling the night away in the arms of the very tall and very British Nigel Towers.

Lindsey Kelly, Spoon Sisters Blog

DEAR FRIENDS,

Tragedy has struck. Poor Lindsey Kelly. The Spoon Sisters fan traveled from Springfield only to see Anne's dress. As it was not on display at the auction, we made arrangements to bring the dress to her hotel room. When we arrived, we found...

CC stopped and fought to find the right words. She always felt compelled to tell her fans the truth, but the truth was not quite known nor did she want to share too many gruesome details with them.

Ms. Kelly suffered from what appeared to be an allergic reaction and died. I only share this news with you because you are family. Please, if you have severe allergies, remember to always carry your EpiPen. I'm renewing my prescription today and will always keep it open.

CC had her own allergies to bees. Thinking of bees made her remember bee pheromone. She continued typing.

Anne is coming over this morning for breakfast. I hope she was able to sleep. I will continue to update you as we have more information. Let's all remember how precious life is and enjoy each day as the gift that it is. I've included some images of Luna and Reina, two lovely black cats that traveled with Lindsey. We hope to find a good home for them. Anne is caring for them now.

Bandit raised his head from his dog bed and growled. "Hush, boo boo, I know how you feel about cats. We're not going to adopt them." He put his head back down.

I must prepare the crepes. They are sure to cheer Anne up. After all, there's nothing that a good meal or a dusty antique can't fix when it comes to Anne. I've shared the recipe with you below. Until next time, dear friends, toodooloo.

As CC started the shower, Anne arrived on her friend's doorstep an hour too early as she was wont to do. She softly tapped on the front door and then let herself in before her knock was finished. As always, CC's Glen Ellyn mid-century trilevel was immaculate, walnut floors gleaming, fresh cut irises and tulips from her early spring garden on the dining room table. Bandit flew down the stairs, barking. "Bandit, it's me." Stopping in his tracks, the dog turned on his wiggle butt. He jumped up and kissed Anne. "Ok, that's enough," she said, pushing him down and swiping red and white fur off her Eileen Fisher blouse. "This is silk."

CC came down the stairs in her bathrobe, stuck her head around the railing. "I'm getting out of the shower." CC glanced at the mantle clock, which read 6:30. "Ingrid's still sleeping." She went back upstairs, dabbing her hair with a towel.

Anne sat at the dining room table, tapping her foot. She couldn't have slept more than an hour or two, but she was ravenous. She looked inside her bag and pulled out some saltines. She nibbled while she waited. Bandit sat waiting for an invitation which he didn't receive.

A few minutes later, Ingrid came down the stairs wearing cutoff blue jeans and a Glen Ellyn Fire Department t-shirt.

"Ingrid, I thought you broke up. . ." Anne said.

She glanced down at her T-shirt. "Oh, force of habit. It's comfortable." She paused. "He offered to help out at the auction. We talked afterwards and decided to see where it goes."

"Oh," Anne said with a smirk.

Ingrid turned on the coffeepot and sat down next to Anne. "CC told me everything that happened last night. How horrible."

"Yes, it was." Anne shuddered, remembering poor Lindsey lying on the floor, her throat swollen. It was a vision she wouldn't quickly forget.

"Do you have any idea what happened?"

"No, no, I don't." Anne paused. "Lindsey Kelly showed up at the auction yesterday and said she came from Springfield to see my dress. According to her card, she was an assistant curator at the Lincoln Museum. CC agreed to bring her the dress, and that's when we found her." Why had CC agreed? If they hadn't gone, she might be able to remove the picture of Lindsey from her head.

"She died of an allergic reaction, but the police didn't say what caused it?" Ingrid asked.

"I was told it wasn't my business." But Anne was making it her business. The poor woman died while waiting for Anne's dress. It was up to Anne to figure out what happened. She owed her that.

"Let's have some breakfast, and then we'll put our heads together." She gave Anne a kiss on the cheek.

Watching Ingrid make coffee, Anne realized how proud she was of her young protégé. It had only been a short while since Ingrid came from Germany to start her journalism career, but Anne had helped her find her true calling—antique hunting. Wanting Ingrid to follow in her footsteps, CC wouldn't admit it. She thought her niece should spend more time at school and less at the antique store, but Anne had wasted so many years at Ebbort Labs hiding behind a microscope while the whole world moved on without her. She had finally gathered the courage to make antique hunting her full-time career. She didn't want Ingrid to make the same mistake and waste years of her life.

CC joined Ingrid in the kitchen and started pulling out bowls. She whisked batter together. "I'm making ham palacsintas."

"Palacsintas? I thought we were having crepes."

"They are Hungarian crepes. These are similar to ones I had in Budapest when I reported on the international steel conference. The chef gave me a tour of his kitchen and shared his recipe with me."

Anne feigned enthusiasm, but as always CC gave a dollar's worth of explanation when a penny would do. "Yes, they sound delicious, and I bet they even taste more delicious than they sound." Her stomach rumbled.

CC smiled and finished up the crepes. She plated them and brought them to the table. Ingrid poured coffee before sitting down.

Anne ate quickly, savoring the warm ham and crispy crepe. So much for her low carb diet. After her third crepe, she stared over at CC.

"What? What are you looking at?"

"What are we going to do?"

"What do you mean?" CC asked.

"About Lindsey?"

"What would you have us do?"

"I think we should go to the Lincoln Museum to find who she was and why she wanted my dress."

"We should leave it up to the police."

"Don't you want to find out what happened? You're a journalist. That's your job."

"I write about the steel industry."

"That's not the point. The point is she came to us, so we owe it to her to find out what happened." Anne pulled out the museum visitor guide from her bag. "It was right in front of me the whole time. I stayed up all night reading books about Mary Todd and her relationship with Keckley. I was searching back in time when I should have been looking into the future."

"What are you talking about?"

"Right here. Next month the museum is hosting an exhibit of Civil War clothing." Anne pointed to a paragraph in the brochure. "My dress. That's why Lindsey wanted my dress. I think it is an authentic Keckley gown."

"That would explain why she wanted to see it." CC cleared the dishes while Anne sat patiently. CC stopped and turned in the doorway from the kitchen. "I think, Anne, it's time we go to Springfield."

Anne's eyes lit up. She felt her shoulders relax. All the stress from the night before was lifted at the mere mention of traveling to see Mary Todd's collection in person. She had read numerous books about the Civil War, the Lincolns, and of course, the fashions of the day. The first lady was a known fashion plate, setting styles, spending money she didn't have on gowns she couldn't afford. Much like. . . No, wait, that was a little too real. "I'll go pack." Anne downed the last of her coffee.

"All right, I'll make arrangements. We can leave in a few days."

On the Road,
Spoon Sisters Blog

DEAR FRIENDS,

    Thanks to all of you who were able to attend the auction yesterday. It was an incredible success. We raised quite a bit of money for the Greater Chicago Family Rescue Fund which helps local at-risk families.

    Anne and I will be traveling to our state capital, Springfield, Illinois, this coming week, to obtain information about Lindsey Kelly. If any of you have requests for items from that area please let us know. I've attached some photos of recent fan finds including a very special find for Carol Zanetta, a Chicago expatriate living in Arizona. She was missing the Windy City and looking for any memorabilia from her childhood. It didn't take long for Anne to get on the trail. She sifted through a recent buy from a fan whose father was a WGN cameraman and found this original Cuddly Dudley stuffed dog, only one of three used on the original Ray Rayner show in the 1960s. Needless to say Carol was very excited to share that dog and its history with her grandchildren.

    Our newest and youngest assistant, nine-year-old Dakota, has proven to be an antique hunting phenom. At a recent estate sale, she bid on this lovely collection of crystal doorknobs. Anne was impressed with their sparkle and wanted to save them in case she can ever rebuild her house, but I have convinced her to place them for sale at the store.

    As you may have noticed, we are now accepting select advertising on our blog and website. This was Ingrid's idea as another way to help with the charity. Our biggest ad contributor is our dear friend Betsy Buttersworth, who has asked me to mention her Easter sale of milk chocolate bunnies. Please stop by her sweet shop located next to our own antique store, Great-Aunt Sybil's

Attic. If you do, please be sure to tell her I sent you and stop by our store to say hi. Thank you all for all of your requests. Anne and I will be working very hard to check them off the list. Please be patient. We have nearly 200,000 blog fans and a million likes on our Facebook page. Each one of you is very dear to us, and we appreciate your support. Until next time, dear friends, too-dooloo.

CC closed her Mac PowerBook with a click. Bandit raised his head. That sound signaled work was done, and it was playtime. CC grabbed his leash, and they headed out the front door to the Prairie Path, their favorite walk, a former route for the electric railway. Bandit stomped over the irises and crocuses that grew along the gravel path. Stopping near a bench, CC admired the milkweed she had helped plant as part of the Monarch Preservation Society. "You know, Bandit, a few hundred more of these plants and a little more effort, we can save the monarchs in Illinois."

Bandit gave her a strange look, opening his mouth, letting a bumblebee fly out. "Boo Bear, we've had this talk. Leave the bees alone." Bandit wiggled his butt and continued his search.

As they walked, she flipped through her iPhone. Since the night, that night, she had set her journalistic eye on Lindsey Kelly. Google, Facebook, LinkedIn accounts fed information that anyone could find, but none of revealed why this woman had come to them. CC contacted a colleague at the Springfield State Register, although reluctant at first because of their history. That history was part of her life that she had not shared with her current boyfriend, Nick. Their relationship had become more serious as of late. For the first time in a long time, she could picture herself married again. In the back of her head, a small voice said, "I hear ya." The voice of her ex-husband John Reeney. She shuddered a bit, then forced her thoughts back to Nick, who had everything in a man she ever wanted. Strength, courage, the ability to make her laugh. They understood each other, and the fact that he was a handsome Glen Ellyn fireman didn't hurt his cause. She shuddered again, but this time for a different reason, and smiled. Bandit stopped and glanced up at her, tongue hanging out of his mouth. "Oh, hush up, Bandit, don't give me that look. You love me, too."

Bandit replied with a quick wiggle butt and then pulled her down the path. His energy was only matched with his determination and his desire to get to the next place, wherever it was. She heard her phone ringing. Staring at the screen, she didn't recognize the number. "Hello."

"CC, is that you?" a male voice said.

"Toby?" CC sat down on a wood bench.

"I was surprised to get your email. It's been what, almost twenty years?"

"Yes, about that, I'd say."

"Right, right. You were dating that Reeney guy."

"Yes, my ex-husband John Reeney."

"Oh, ex?" Toby's voice suddenly sounded very enthused.

CC began regretting contacting him. "Yes, thank you for calling. As I said in my email, I'm trying to track down information on Lindsey Kelly."

"So, how you been, CC? Are you still at the steel mag?"

"Yes, Toby."

"I'm still at the Register. I'm managing editor now. Single. Can you believe it? After all these years? Never married?"

CC was quiet for a second, rubbed her forehead. It had taken her a while but she realized she had a tendency to choose the wrong man. Something about Toby and her ex and the list went on, drawing her to men that needed fixing. Maybe that's why she finally fell in love with Nick. There was nothing to fix. "So were you able to find anything about Lindsey in the local paper? There must be something about her associated with the museum."

"I met her a few times when I was covering events at the museum. Before she became assistant curator, she consulted with the museum on special events. She came from Bloomington, Illinois."

"Bloomington?"

"She owned a vintage dress shop with her sister in Bloomington. Her sister still runs it. Let me see here." CC could hear shuffling of papers. "I printed it out. She sourced costumes for theaters, TV, and movies. She tracked down original costumes and props. The museum hired her to help with staging dresses."

"She lives, lived, in Springfield?" CC interrupted.

"Yes. Are you planning a trip down? I'd love to show you around. At least let's meet for drinks. I'm part owner in a local brewery."

"I have to check my schedule with work, but I appreciate the offer."

"I'll email you everything I have. Photos and her bio. I'll keep an eye open for anything else," he said. "Why are you so interested in Lindsey?"

"It's about a dress. Thank you so much, Toby." CC hung up.

Anne Hillstrom, Spoon Sister Blog

D*EAR FRIENDS,*
   I am taking over for CC and wanted to share some of my recent finds with you. Don't tell CC. Let's keep this between us as she has been discouraging me from shopping as of late. I picked up these vintage cow and sunflower salt and pepper shakers. I haven't been able to discover their provenance, but they appear to be mid-century. Won't they be cute on the tables at the café? I'm very excited about this Victorian-era dress form with a cage. The base is iron, the cage metal is adjustable, and the fabric-covered figure is adjustable. Of course, I bought it with myself in mind. I can use it to display my Keckley dress at Great-Aunt Sybil's Attic. I've read so many of your comments about poor Lindsey Kelly, I want you to know that I'm on the case. I will not rest until I know what happened to her. This I promise you.

Anne sat back on the chrome kitchen chair. She eyed the copper teakettle on the stove but realized there was no time for tea.

CC is preparing for our trip to Springfield, and now my dear friends, I also need to pack. I will write to you from the road. The game is afoot. Anne.

Entering the antique store, she heard a commotion from upstairs. A crash, a yelp followed by a hiss. She flew up the stairs. Greeting her were three white cats and one black. She stood momentarily pondering the numbers, counting them on her fingers and then saw the broken bag of flour spread across the kitchen table and floor. Sassy licked her paws. Luna was covered in flour. "Oh my goodness." Anne bent down and picked her up. Brushing off the flour, she sent a cloud of dust flying. Luna rubbed her head against Anne's shoulder, leaving flour all over her dress. Sassy and Sybil sat perfectly still as if not knowing what had happened.

Reina whimpered. Anne picked her up. "Sybil, Sassy, these are our guests. I expect you to treat them as such."

Turning her back, Sassy pranced away followed by Sybil. After Luna was returned to her natural state, Anne started packing. Eying her dress, she considered wearing it but then thought better of it. She piled her vintage dresses into a vintage Louis Vuitton trunk, the only piece remaining from her recent trip to Paris. As money often did with Anne, her fortune had come and gone.

There was a soft tap on the door. She opened it to see Ingrid standing at the top of the steps. "Come in. Come in. I'm in the middle of packing," Anne said, blocking the path into the antique store with her foot so the cats couldn't escape.

"Anne, I wanted to talk to you about your trip. I've been Googling the Lincoln Museum, and I'd love to see it," Ingrid said.

Anne took Ingrid by the hand and sat her in one of the wing-back chairs by the fire. She then sat next to her. "Oh, Ingrid, what an adventure we could have. We could literally spend days wandering the museum, the antique malls, and historic sites. But CC feels we need you to manage the store. It wouldn't be fair to our fans to close it."

Ingrid's face fell. Her coneflower summer blue eyes glistened slightly. The beautiful, young twenty-year-old that sat before Anne was more than her protégé. She was a younger sister, not much younger, but still a younger sister. Anne had always wished for a sister growing up. The closest she came was her cousin Suzanne, but to have had a full-time best friend, confident, mischief maker—that was Anne's truest wish. When she was just seven and had started reading *Anne of Green Gables,* she imagined Anne, the other Anne, as her sister. And then Nancy Drew became her sister. She read every book in order. It wasn't until this very moment Anne realized what was missing in her life. Family. Her closest relative, Aunt Sybil, who had been a mother to her, was gone. Suzanne had her own life and family. Anne leapt out of the chair, hugged Ingrid, and then pulled back. Ingrid appeared surprised.

"What's wrong, Anne?"

Anne pulled a lace handkerchief out of her pocket and dabbed her eyes. "Oh, nothing. I really wish you could come with us. How about this? How about if I FaceTime you while we walk around the museum?"

"Can you do that?"

"I'm sure it'll be fine."

"Since we're talking about the store, I was wondering if we could give Dakota more responsibility. She really helped at the auction, and she's been helping bus the tables at the Bee's Knees."

"Of course. What'd you have in mind?"

"Actually it's Dakota's idea. She wants to start a blog for kids about antiquing. She thought she could start with things like Barbie dolls, Hot Wheels, things that kids would not only collect but would play with."

"That's a wonderful idea."

"She'd like to hold a special kids' day sale at the store. I already talked to Betsy, and she said she would donate cupcakes."

"Buttersworth," Anne muttered under her breath.

"Excuse me?"

"Nothing."

"I wanted to check with you before I said yes."

"Of course. In fact, hold on." Anne ran into her bedroom, opened the barn door closet door. Items spilled out on to the floor around her. She stood on her tippy toes and retrieved a hatbox, sending boxes tumbling around it. "Coming," she yelled back into the living room. She placed the hatbox on the small round table between the chairs. A lovely flowered hatbox from the now-defunct Charles A. Stevens' store. The box was careworn but had special meaning as it passed between CC and Anne for years. She carefully lifted the lid. She held up a vintage tin spinning toy.

"Oh, Anne, that's so cute."

"Yes, let me see." She rummaged through the box, pulling out spinning tops. "These are 1950s Ohio art and come in several sizes and shapes. I think it would be perfect for the sale." Anne held the box a moment. "I hate to part with them." She hesitated before finally handing them over to Ingrid. "You tell Dakota they're from me with my blessing."

"That's perfect. You know, Anne, you're all Dakota talks about. She wants to grow up to be just like you."

Anne thought of the little blue-eyed blonde girl who could have been Anne at nine years old. Like Anne she was an only child. "Ingrid, before we leave on our trip, what do you say you and Dakota come over for dinner and we can talk about the sale?"

"That'd be lovely, Anne."

A crash came from the kitchen. They both jumped and ran into the small galley. One of Anne's bone china dogs mysteriously had fallen from the shelf above the kitchen table and broke into a thousand shards, inches away from Sassy who was curled up on the corner of the table. From behind the brass coffee grinders on the shelf, the wagging of a black tail could be seen. Anne looked at Ingrid. "We're going to have to talk about the cats and how to take care of them."

Guess Who's Coming for Dinner, Spoon Sisters Blog

*D*EAR FRIENDS,
        What a lovely dinner we had tonight," CC typed. *"Anne has been the perfect hostess. We were honored to have Betsy Buttersworth with us. She has been a delight. The topic of conversation was the upcoming children's sale at Great-Aunt Sybil's Attic. While Anne clears the dishes, I am taking time to write. I feel I've been neglecting you, our loyal fans, as of late. I've listed a few finds from the past week. You must forgive me. I am so scattered. I have so much on my mind. I feel that I have been pushed down a road. My comfortable life as a journalist and antique hunter has dulled my intuitive edges. I find that we are on a journey, Anne and I—evolving. Please forgive my drifting. Once again, I have had so much on my mind as of late.*

CC glanced up at Anne who was clearing the table.

"Can't that wait?" Anne asked, balancing a stack of her Royal Albert china. Not her best china but certainly fitting for a casual gathering of good friends and Buttersworth. Anne was still perturbed that Ingrid invited Buttersworth. "Buttersworth," she muttered.

CC quickly typed.

Until next time, dear friends."

She closed her laptop.

The small apartment barely fit six at the dining room table. Anne carried out a tray of petit fours Buttersworth had brought. It calmed Anne's nerves a bit. She placed them on the table and sat at the opposite end of Buttersworth.

"Anne, I think you've done a wonderful job with your flat," Betsy said.

This annoyed Anne to no limit. As of late, Buttersworth had

started using British phrases. Anne swore she had developed an English accent. Her latest chocolatier was British. Buttersworth went through chocolatiers quicker than she did ex-husbands. "Thank you. It's just temporary until I find a house."

"I know how difficult that can be. I have four houses. Each one carefully chosen for its location, and of course, there's climate to consider. One simply must have a summer and winter home. There's the downtown flat,"

As Buttersworth droned on, Anne quietly tapped her foot under the table, counting each tap not realizing her mouth was moving as she counted to ten. Caroline broke the tension. "Anne, Dakota wanted to thank you for letting her have the kid's sale at the store. That's really sweet of you." "You're quite welcome. Dakota's part of the family. She's important to us and the store." Anne thought for a moment. "Speaking of the sale, maybe we should go downstairs and discuss the set up." She stood.

Her guests followed her downstairs into the closed store, standing around her in a semicircle. "We can move the furniture out to the corners and set up some tables here in the center." Anne spread her arms out, picturing the display. Ingrid and CC set up a few folding tables. Anne placed her finger on her chin. "Let me see, the box of tops." She ran to the kitchenette and grabbed the box.

"Oh, and?" She ran to a cabinet, reached inside and pulled out a mischievous looking gorilla popping out of a box that read, "Magilla Gorilla for sale." Anne took the gorilla out of the box and handed it to Dakota. "You're much too young to remember this cartoon. This is a 1964 Magilla Gorilla Toonykin musical wind-up toy and its original box. Notice the brightness of the colors on the box and on the toy. This adds to its value. Here's something interesting; count the little dots on his nose."

Dakota counted aloud. "Eighteen, Anne?"

"Yes, eighteen is the correct number, but if you ever find one and you count seventeen, buy it immediately. There was a brief problem with production. The ones with seventeen dots are very valuable. For this one, a good price would be sixty dollars."

Dakota squealed. "I'm going to tell everybody."

"It's very important to educate the young ones." Anne patted Dakota on her head. Next she pulled out some little toy soldiers no more than two inches tall. "Dakota, these are Barclay lead soldiers. This one with the bazooka is from the 1940s. These two with rifles are somewhere in that era also." Anne thought for a moment. "We're not going to sell these though, because they're made of lead. Make a mental note: If you find these at a store, their resale value is about twenty dollars each but better not sell to kids." She put them back in her glass display case. Anne fluttered about the store searching high and low for anything appropriate for kids. After scrounging in the depths of a console, she came out bearing a toy tank. She turned it over. "See, Dakota, it says 'made in Japan,' Japanese tin toys are quite popular." She rubbed the wheels on the table, and it took off. "It's called a friction tank. You give the wheels a good spin, and it takes off. I would value it at fifteen dollars . It's from the late 1960s."

"I have a couple boxes at home of toys I've been collecting. None of them as nice as yours, Anne, but hopefully they will sell," Dakota said.

"Ingrid will help you price everything." Anne turned to Ingrid. "If there is anything else you find that you think would be good for the sale, go ahead," she whispered.

"Yes, and Anne, guess what." Dakota said, her face lighting up. "Betsy, I mean Miss Buttersworth—"

Betsy interrupted. "Dakota, you can call me Betsy."

"Betsy is going to let me bake the cupcakes for the sale. She's teaching me how to make caramels."

"Really? That's very interesting." Anne wasn't sure about how she felt about her rival helping her young protégé.

"She's a natural. In fact, when she gets tired of working at the antique store, she has a job at my sweet shop. She's aces," Betsy said.

Aces, that's what Nigel would say. That's what Nigel did say. And Betsy knew it. It was her little dig. Buttersworth had stolen Nigel from her, she had stolen him back. And then whatever adventure he was on stole him from the two of them. "Dakota, I think it's great to learn a manual labor trade like baking in case you decide not to go to college."

Caroline interrupted. "Oh, no, Dakota has a college fund. She's been putting all her earnings from the store into the fund, and I've been contributing."

"Speaking of dessert, should we head back upstairs?" Anne asked, leading the way. Buttersworth hesitated as if she knew she had worn out her welcome.

"And Betsy too," Dakota added.

Anne couldn't argue with the young girl. Everyone followed her back to her small apartment, including Betsy, who smiled. Anne took a bite of a petit four. Then she took a second, then a third. CC put her hand on Anne's leg to stop the tapping. "CC, Ingrid tells me you are headed to Springfield to the Lincoln Museum," Betsy said. "I've spent several Christmases in Springfield at the Governor's Mansion, and I was at the museum for its inaugural ball. It's lovely."

"That's right."

"Ingrid told me about Lindsey Kelly. It seems you and Anne have become quite the detectives," Betsy said, raising her teacup.

Anne couldn't hold back any longer. "It's our responsibility. You can make light of it, but yes, in our own way we are detectives if being a detective means searching for the truth."

"Better to let the police handle it. Haven't you had enough excitement in your life?" Betsy asked.

CC quickly changed the conversation. "I have an old friend who works at the Springfield Register. He's going to show us around, open some doors for us. The Lincoln Museum would be a good connection for the antique store."

"Plus don't forget the dress," Anne added.

"Oh, yes, the your ball gown. The one thing I couldn't buy and apparently Lindsey couldn't either," Betsy said, setting her teacup down with a clink.

Anne stood up, crossed her arms over chest. "Coffee? Would anyone like more coffee?"

"I wouldn't mind a bit more cuppa with my afters," Betsy said.

Anne sighed. "That's it."

CC put a restraining hand on Anne's arm as she moved toward Betsy's end of the table.

"Anne, why don't you get the dress so you can show Betsy?" CC said.

Anne smiled a crooked smile. She came back a few minutes later wearing the dress without the hoops. She did a quick spin as the skirt and its belt of fringe chased after her. Luna and Reina chased after the skirt. She brushed up against Betsy as she walked by the fold-up table crammed between the couch and wing back chairs. Betsy admired the silk, rubbing it between her fingers. "It's an original Elizabeth Keckley?"

"We don't know that for sure yet," CC said.

"Look, there's a bloodstain." Anne lifted the bottom of the skirt. "This dress has seen battle. Maybe it was worn by a field nurse, patching up poor fallen soldiers or maybe by a rich New York debutante caught in the middle of a duel. The possibilities are endless, and that's why we have to go to Springfield. We believe it was part of the Mary Todd Lincoln collection."

"And more importantly, we can find out why Lindsey came for the dress," CC said.

Anne stopped for a moment, realizing the gravity of the adventure. She had learned to put such gravity to the side, to lock it away not to think about it. A woman had died, and her last desire was to see the dress that Anne was wearing at this moment. She stared down at the bloodstain. Blood had been shed at least twice now for this dress. "Of course, CC, of course." Anne went back into the bedroom and changed.

At the end of the evening, Anne thanked everyone for coming, even Betsy. She and CC sat by the fire, sipping tea from the Doyle teapot. Lines had been drawn as they were during the Civil War days of the dress. White cats on one side of the fireplace and black cats on the other. Both asleep yet aware of the enemy. "What are you going to do about these four?" CC asked.

Anne put her teacup down. "Oh, I thought Ingrid told you. She's going to stay here watching everyone. In fact, Dakota's going to sleep over the night before the sale."

"That will work. My brother will watch Bandit. I guess there's no reason for us not to go."

"What's wrong? You seem reluctant."

CC hesitated. "My friend at the paper that will be helping us out."

Anne sipped her tea, looking over the cup at CC.

"It's Toby."

Anne choked on her tea. She cleared her throat and put the teacup down. "Toby?"

"Yes, that Toby."

"How do you feel about seeing him again?"

"It's been so long and we were both so young. I made my choice, right or wrong."

Anne thought about her choice, John Reeney, and hoped CC would never make another choice like that again. "Are you going to tell Nick?"

CC sighed. "There's nothing to tell. Toby is just a memory. Those years are just memories. I'm asking a colleague to help us out. It's not personal, it's business."

"He asked you to marry him."

CC was quiet. The fire crackled, casting a warm glow over the room. Luna kicked in her sleep. "I better tell Nick, huh?"

Anne nodded.

CC glanced at her watch. "It's getting late. I still have to pack." She stood up.

"Let me walk you out," Anne said.

"No need."

"Ok. Text me when you get home."

"Sure, Anne." CC left and Anne locked the door. After dressing for bed, she peeled back the down comforter. All four cats jumped up and found a spot on the pillow top. Anne stared up though the skylight. Clouds floated over the moon, leading the room into almost complete darkness. She was exhausted, but sleep had not come easy as of late. The image of Lindsey haunted her dreams. She secretly blamed herself and the dress. What if she had sold the dress at the auction? Would Lindsey still be alive? What if? What if? Those two words spun around her head like one of the tin tops she had given Dakota. As the last what if drifted out of her head, she woke with a start. She sat straight up in the bed. All four cats were already at attention. "Was that a dream?" she asked.

Sassy turned her head around as if to answer no. Anne listened.

It was not a dream. Someone was rattling the front door, testing its ability to remain locked. "Oh, no," she said. "Where'd I put my phone?" It began to rain. The drops on the skylight pinged like pebbles against a brick wall. She listened hard, trying to make out any other sounds. She slipped into her slippers and headed down the steps, the old stairs creaking under her feet. The clock on the microwave glowed three o'clock. "I must have dreamt it." She flipped the switch on the kitchenette wall, but there was nothing. She tried again and again but still nothing. Against CC's advice, she hadn't upgraded the fuse box to breakers.

Reaching around for a weapon, all she could find was a kitchen knife. No, not a knife—too many bad things happen with knives. She tiptoed into the storefront. The first thing she saw was an antique blunderbuss. Taking it out of the display case, she thought how silly it was to hold a 300-year-old gun that wasn't loaded and wouldn't work even if it were. She clutched it to her chest as lightning struck. The stained glass window in the front door illuminated. Light crashed through onto the floor outlining a shadow. Screaming, she dropped the gun. Aunt Sybil watched from above the cash register. "Aunt Sybil," Anne said out loud. She was fearless. What would she do? Anne knew what she would do. Picking up the gun, she walked to the front door. Out of habit, she flipped the light switch by the door, and the Edison lights hanging in the front window flickered and then gave a soft yellow glow. "Not all the fuses blown," Anne whispered. With eyes barely open, she peered out the window. The street was empty. She checked the door. It was still locked. Moving the large Victorian chaise in front of the door to block entry, she let out a deep sigh and flopped onto it. She felt something heavy on her lap and jumped out of the seat, screaming. Sassy went flying with a loud scream of her own.

On the Road,
Spoon Sisters Blog

*D*EAR FRIENDS,
CC typed, sipping her first cup of coffee. *Today, Anne and I embark on our road trip to Springfield. We plan to stop at the Lincoln Museum. I haven't been there since the new museum opened, so I am looking forward to seeing it. We will be posting pictures of finds along the way, checking items off our list and most importantly, we are going to find out more about Lindsey Kelly. I've been troubled by the dress and Miss Kelly's unfortunate passing. There are so many pieces of this puzzle left unfound. Thank you all for the kind comments about Miss Kelly.* CC took another sip and wrote. *I promise to keep you up to date and blog every day of our trip but for now I'm sure Anne is waiting so until next time, dear friends, toodooloo.*

After a sleepless night during which Anne ate leftover frozen Christmas cookies, flipped through infomercials, and skimmed through Facebook, she greeted Ingrid. "What's going on?" Ingrid asked, glancing around the room at the mound of candy wrappers and newspapers.

"I couldn't sleep last night." Anne finished packing her Vera Bradley bag with everything she thought she needed for their trip. "Thank you so much for watching the cats." Then Anne handed Ingrid the key to her Mercedes SUV.

"Really, Anne?"

"Of course. What if you find a great buy for the store or have an emergency or something? Besides CC insisted we take her VW. It's become our official road trip vehicle." With a flourish, Anne wrapped her vintage Burberry silk scarf around her neck. Lindsey would have loved this scarf. She, too, seemed to be a collector of fine scarves.

She went over to the window seat where all four cats were watching the early spring morning bird fest. A particularly fat robin had been antagonizing Sassy for two weeks. Anne picked up Reina and Luna. "You two, behave, for Ingrid. We're going to find you a good home, I promise." She nuzzled both their necks. Then she picked up Sybil and whispered, "Treat our guests kindly."

Sassy refused to turn her gaze from the robin. She did not like when Anne left for more than a day. She had communicated this with Anne on several occasions, but Anne still did not understand.

"Come on, Sassy, don't be that way. It won't be for more than a few days, I promise. And you love Ingrid."

Sassy let out a low growl. She was not amused. Anne picked her up and hugged her anyway. Sassy rubbed her head against Anne's neck. "Thank you, Sassy, I love you, too." Anne looked out to see the smiling face of the lime-green-and-white 1968 VW bus. She kissed Ingrid and grabbed her bags, only three this time. Ingrid followed behind carrying the dress in a special Louis Vuitton garment bag. They loaded up the VW, hugged Ingrid one last time, and then took off.

"I thought we'd stop in Bloomington on the way and speak with Lindsey's sister," CC said.

"That's a good idea. I wanted to stop by there anyway. We have a fan at the local antique store. She asked us to drop in." Anne pulled out her iPhone. "It's called Bellwood Antiques." She shoved her phone in front of CC's face, blocking her view of the road.

CC waved her away. "Not now. I'm driving," she said. "We'll stop."

Scrolling through the photo gallery on the website, Anne admired the china and the crystal chandelier, while swiping past the industrial footlockers. "There's also the Bloomington Antique Mall. Maybe we should spend a couple days in Bloomington."

"No, it's too late to change our reservations in Springfield. I prepaid to get a better rate." CC hesitated before adding, "Anne, remember a woman died."

She thought for a moment. CC was right. Now was not the

time for frivolity though shopping did relieve her mind and help her think. Often her best ideas came when she was scrounging through antiques. "You're right." Anne pictured the two homeless cats, Luna and Reina, currently guests in her house. Anne put down her iPhone. Shopping didn't hold quite the same appeal.

However, that changed when they reached the main drive into the downtown section of Bloomington. Anne saw the shop windows advertising antiques and felt the familiar twinge of searching for a great deal. She couldn't miss this opportunity. Who knew when she might be in this town again? Checking her watch, she saw they had a few hours before the shops closed. Anne understood the importance of keeping stores open late for people who had full-time jobs. Great-Aunt Sybil's Attic stayed open late.

CC pulled into the parking lot of Kelly's Vintage, a turn-of-the-century Victorian, freshly painted Pepto Bismol pink with gray accents. Anne barely waited for CC to stop the engine before getting out of the car and running inside. What was once the sitting room was now filled with antique dress forms, decorated with beautiful taffeta, silk and lace.

Through all items, Anne spotted a circa 1920s olive green velvet cloche hat with a bow. "I've been looking for a driving hat like this." Without trying it on, she brought it up to the counter.

The woman at the register admired the hat before wrapping it in rose-printed tissue paper. "That came in the other day. I really like it so did our owner. She was having a hard time parting with it."

"I can understand why." Anne paid for her purchase before wandering through the rest of the store.

Then she admired a 1930s peach silk evening gown. "This is a Mainbocher," she said after reading the label. "You remember that exhibit we saw of his work at the Chicago History Museum?"

Stepping back, CC took a picture for their blog with Anne posed next to the evening gown.

"Wow, these are fabulous." Anne stared at the 1940s WAVE uniforms, which took up another wall. The gray seersucker dress featured a gored skirt and matching jacket with the Chicago fashion designer's distinctive design of a rounded collar layered over a pointed lapel.

"Those are also Mainbocher," a voice said from down the hall. The girls turned to see a distinguished young Clark Gable standing in the archway. The sunlight crashing through the stained glass window illuminated the fact that he could be a model on a Harlequin cover.

CC blinked her eyes to make sure he wasn't a mannequin. He was dressed in gray flannel cuffed trousers, white button-down shirt, white and brown spectator oxford shoes, and brown leather jacket. He smiled, glancing down at this outfit. "I had to try it on. It's for a World War II movie about the Battle of the Bulge. The WAVE costumes are for the same movie."

Anne didn't like the Battle of the Bulge as she consistently fought her own battle.

"I'm Cliff Landry. I'm the owner," he said.

"Of Kelly? Of Kelly's Dresses?" Anne asked.

"Part owner," he replied. "Kelly is my wife's maiden name."

"Oh, I'm so sorry about your wife," CC said.

"You know Connie?"

"Connie?" Anne asked.

Lindsey Kelly entered the room, wearing a vintage Yves St. Laurent black pencil skirt and cranberry cashmere twin set. Anne and CC gasped.

"May I help you?" she asked.

CC cleared her throat, not saying anything.

"I'm Connie, the owner of this shop. May I help you?" she said, holding out her hand.

CC reached out her hand to shake Connie's.

Anne interrupted. "I'm sorry, but you are the spitting image of…" Then she stopped in mid-sentence.

Connie frowned. "You knew my sister, my twin?"

CC placed her other hand on top of Connie's. "Yes. We're so sorry for your loss."

Connie removed her hand from between CC's. "How did you know Lindsey?"

"We only met your sister briefly. She came to us about a dress."

"What dress is that?"

"A dress I found in a resale shop. I believe it is an Elizabeth Keckley gown," Anne said.

"If Lindsey was interested in it, I would like to see it," she said.

"Let me get it." Anne ran out to the car and carefully brought in the Louis Vuitton garment bag. After heading back into the store, she unzipped it and pulled out the blue silk dress.

Connie ran the fabric through her fingers. She flipped over the back and examined the hand-sewn label. She retrieved a loupe from behind the counter and studied the beadwork. "These appear to be jet beads, and the workmanship is true to the period. See? Each bead is individually drilled and hand-sewn to the dress, but this pattern is very unusual. On most dresses from this period, the beading would be more symmetrical. It appears as if some of the beads are missing, but I don't see any missing stitches. There's so many of them. This would have taken months of manual labor. I've never seen a Keckley dress with this much detail before. This dress would have cost a fortune."

"Is it authentic?" Anne asked. "Is it an authentic Keckley ball gown?"

Connie laughed. "This wouldn't have been a ball gown. The neckline is too high. Necklines on ball gowns in the 1860s were lower. And this dress would have had a longer train. This was an afternoon dress, unusual because it's so elaborate but an afternoon dress nonetheless."

"Is it authentic?" Anne repeated.

"It looks to be about the right era and fabric. If you want a second opinion, I'd speak with the curator at the Lincoln Museum, Rachel Contraldes. She hired Lindsey to help develop the Mary Todd Lincoln collection. That's when Lindsey left me to run the store by myself years ago. That's the last I saw of my sister."

"Oh?"

"My sister and I had a falling out about her leaving the store. Now I regret not speaking with her," Connie said.

"I'm sorry to hear that," Anne said.

"We're actually on our way to Springfield to meet with Rachel," CC said.

Connie continued her examination of the dress. "I'd be interested in buying it from you."

"It's not for sale," Anne said, scooping it up and putting it back in the bag. "By the way, we have Reina and Luna."

Connie gave her a blank look.

"Your sister's cats," Anne said. "We can bring them to you."

"I don't like cats." Connie shuddered.

"Thank you for your time. We appreciate it. Again, I'm sorry for your loss." CC smiled.

Connie returned the smile. "We're holding a memorial service for Lindsey at Wakefield Cemetery tomorrow morning if you're still in town."

"Of course. We'll do our best to make it," CC said.

Connie took CC's hand in hers. Her lips shivered as she tried to manage a smile.

Anne and CC left the store, heading back to the VW. Anne whispered, "I think we should go tomorrow to pay our respects."

CC nodded. "Let's take a break from the dress and stop at the antique store you mentioned."

"Yes, I nearly forgot." Anne put the address in her phone. "Gladys read about the dress in the blog post you wrote and sent me an email about Keckley."

A short while later, they arrived at Bellwood Antiques, located in a former high school. Anne couldn't wait to step inside. CC followed. Gazing around, Anne could not contain her enthusiasm. This was her venue, her natural habitat. Dusty rows of china, crystal, porcelain, ornate furniture, and gilt pictures frames. Anne smiled at CC, who pulled out her reporter's notebook and ran her finger along the fan list. "Perfect. Clarence from Knoxville is looking for original parts for his Mini Cooper." She pointed to the shelf full of speedometers and tachometers, one proudly displaying the Union Jack with the words Mini underneath it. They walked down the hallways that once held teenagers scurrying to class at the ring of a bell. Each classroom instead of being filled with young minds was full of old treasures.

Anne felt at home amongst the cluttered shelves. The first classroom held mostly wooden chairs, small cabinets, and a hodgepodge of 1940s furniture and knick knacks. Nothing on their fan list. They strolled down the halls filled with lockers, feeling sixteen again. Stopping to examine glassware, china, sports memorabilia, and Illinois State University collectibles. They stopped in front of the double gym doors, which had a sign reading, "Vintage jewelry show." Anne giggled like a schoolgirl, fan list forgotten.

The inside of the gym was crowded with tables of dealers displaying racks and glass cases filled with baubles. Anne stopped to admire an antique Art Deco gold German-made ruby-enamel tropical fish brooch. The tag was flipped over so she couldn't read the price, one of Anne's pet peeves. She tapped the glass loud enough for the old woman sitting on the folding chair behind the case to hear. The woman seemed annoyed at being summoned by a woman thirty years her junior until she realized whom it was. Anne thought she looked old enough and angry enough to have been the school librarian when it opened in the 1950s. She was rail thin, with her grey hair pulled tightly in a bun. Her horn-rimmed glasses hung by a chain around her neck. She wore a beige pantsuit which was as bland as her expression. Anne tapped louder. The woman set her book down with a thud and came over. "Excuse me, would you mind not tapping on the glass?"

Anne smiled, counting to ten behind her teeth, her tongue barely moving. "I'm so sorry. It's just that I'm very, very interested in this brooch. As you can see, there is no way possible of knowing its price. I'm sure the price is reasonable."

"I'm sorry. Do I know you?"

"I'm somewhat of a celebrity in the antique world. My name is Anne Hillstrom. So glad to meet you."

The woman smiled. "Oh my goodness. I'm so embarrassed. I should have recognized you immediately," she said putting on her glasses. "I'm blind without these things. I'm Gladys. I wrote to you about Elizabeth Keckley's book."

"Of course, Gladys, so nice to meet you. You never mentioned anything about your beautiful jewelry."

"No, this was quite last minute. I hadn't planned on selling any of it. Let me show you the brooch." Gladys adjusted her glasses on her nose, peered down into the cabinet, and then back up at Anne. She let out an audible sigh and reached into her pocket, removing a small key and sliding open the case. Retrieving the brooch, she examined the tag that dangled from it. "I have it marked $182."

"Can I see it?" Anne asked.

Gladys handed her the brooch. Anne examined it carefully, searching for marring in the enamel, chips, or other signs of wear. It was in nearly perfect condition. "Do you know anything about it?" Anne asked.

"My grandmother bought it in Paris in 1925," the librarian said.

"That's really interesting. Did she attend the Exposition International des Arts Decoratifs et Industriels Modernes?" Anne asked, naming the fair that was credited with starting the Art Deco movement.

The librarian managed a small cooked smile. "You're familiar with the exposition?"

"Oh yes, I've studied it quite a bit." CC appeared behind Anne, happy to teach the teacher. She took the brooch. "There were 15,000 exhibitors from 20 different countries and 16 million people visited during its seven-month run. The exposition was dedicated to decorative arts by the Society of Decorative Artists including Eugene Grasset and Hector Guimard. The Society of Decorative Artists lobbied the Chamber of Deputies in 1912 but the exposition was delayed until 1925 due to World War I," CC said.

"We're talking about the brooch now," Anne said, taking the brooch back.

"Oh yes, of course. It's quite lovely."

"By the way, my name is Gladys." She nodded to CC.

"Gladys is the fan who wrote to me," Anne said.

"Maybe you can help me with this piece. It's another brooch that belonged to my grandmother." Pulling another piece out of the case, she handed it to Anne.

Anne studied the small Egyptian scarab brooch. "Egyptian revival," she said.

"Egyptian revival pieces were popular in the Art Deco era," CC said. "Partly because of the discovery of King Tut's tomb in 1922."

"Are all these from your grandmother's collection?" Anne asked.

Gladys' smile dropped. "Yes, they're all I have left of her."

"Do you mind me asking how you could part with them?" Anne pictured her overflowing storage locker filled in part with many of her Great-Aunt Sybil's things. She had a difficult time parting with these treasured items, lasting memories of her now-gone relative.

Gladys took the scarab brooch back from Anne and locked it in the case. She looked about the crowded room and then said, "Let's talk outside." Anne and CC followed her out past the crowds to what was once a recess yard with a basketball court. Gladys sat on a worn-out metal bench. Anne and CC sat next to her. Gladys looked up at the old school building. "I retired five years ago. I started as the school librarian in 1958 right after the school opened."

Anne thought she is a librarian. She was proud of her deductive skills.

"Best years of my life were spent in this school, but the school and I both outlived our purpose."

Anne put her hand on top of Gladys' hand. "I wouldn't say that, Gladys. I'm sure you touched a lot of lives. And now you're sharing your wonderful heirlooms with people, and those will touch a lot of lives also."

"I was hoping by selling my grandmother's jewelry I could help fund a reading program for the Bloomington area kids. The school system doesn't have as many resources as it used to. And a lot of the kids are reading below grade level."

"That's terrible," CC said. "Can't the city help fund a program like that?"

"No, the school system has a large deficit. They've cut after-school programs, most of the music and sport programs are gone. There's only enough funding for core curriculum. Some schools don't even have a proper library."

"That's unimaginable. Every child should own a book. It gives them not just a sense of pride but a sense of accomplishment," CC said.

Gladys started crying. Anne pulled a lace handkerchief out of her bag and handed it to Gladys. "Thank you," she said dabbing at her eyes. "I don't mean to be such a blabbering idiot."

"No, don't be ridiculous." Anne patted her hand. "Gladys, take a deep breath."

Gladys did. "I have boxes and boxes of books in the basement, gathering dust. All the classics, Stevenson, Irving, Updike, Steinbeck, Frost. Hawthorne. Wyss. Verne."

"I love *Swiss Family Robinson*. I read it as girl," CC said.

Gladys sniffled. "Think of all the tree forts never built, all the roads not taken, children not inspired by the wonders in those pages."

"I've always wanted to travel to Prince Edward Island and have tea with Anne," Anne said, picturing herself running through Anne's White Way of Delight, and then sipping tea and raspberry cordial with Diana and Anne in Green Gables.

"I imagine myself with Captain Nemo at the helm," CC said. "Circumnavigating the world under the oceans."

"We have to help."

"Yes, of course, Anne."

"Can you show us the books?"

Gladys managed a smile. They followed her back into the building, through the rear of the gym, down a hallway, down a stairway. They reached the basement, with one fluorescent light flickering over the metal door and a metal cage over the window. Gladys opened the door. It smelled damp and dark with just a hint of mystery. When she flipped the switch on the wall, several overhead fluorescent lights angrily flickered and then illuminated the storage room, which was packed with hundreds of boxes. Anne and CC eagerly opened the boxes as if it were Christmas morning, pulling out books. Some editions dated back to the 1950s. "*Blackboard Jungle*," Anne said, holding up the book.

"An original *Catcher in the Rye*." CC held the book up.

Anne grabbed it. "This must be valuable."

"Gladys, why aren't these books donated to the local library?"

"The same reason the school was shut down—due to lack of funding and lack of interest."

"That's disgraceful. Gladys we have some friends I know who would be happy to help out."

"Why don't you hang onto your grandmother's pieces? Give us some time." Anne added though she still longed for the fish brooch.

"Really? You're willing to help?"

Anne hugged the old woman. She could feel her bony shoulders through her polyester beige pantsuit jacket. As Anne lingered, a burst of light exploded in her head, part premonition, part realization that this could be her, alone, looking for a purpose. She thought about Nigel. She opened her eyes. "Give us a little time, Gladys."

Help Wanted, Spoon Sisters Blog

DEAR FRIENDS,
CC typed. *Anne and I are on a road trip to Springfield. Our stopover in Bloomington at Bellwood Antiques was filled with many great finds. As always we're checking off our request list, and we will be contacting some of you individually. More importantly we met a wonderful fan named Gladys, a former librarian in the very building that the antique store was located in.* Anne watched over CC's shoulder as she typed.

"Tell them about the brooches. Tell them about the books," Anne urged.

"Anne, please," CC said, before returning to typing.

Gladys is selling her grandmother's Art Deco brooches to help fund a reading program for underprivileged children in the Bloomington area. As in many parts of the country, the school system is underfunded. Gladys saved all the books from the school's library, but she needs help. Not just financial help but she needs people willing to donate their time to deliver books to area children, to help tutor them, and to instill a love of reading that is missing in this age of social media and video games. If you know anyone in the Bloomington area who is able to help, please let me know. Perhaps some of you are retired educators yourself or share the love of reading. Tomorrow Anne and I plan to look for a space to store the books and perhaps tutor kids after school. Until then, dear friends, toodooloo for now.

CC clicked the PowerBook closed with a snap.

Anne sat down at the tiny workspace in the hotel room across from her, sipping her Diet Coke. "You know that the scarab brooch was solid gold?"

"Yes, I noticed."

"I think it'd be worth thousands, maybe even more." Anne had researched gold scarab brooches on auction websites.

"Yes, but it was her grandmother's."

"If we helped her sell it, isn't it more important for her to have the money for her program?"

"I have faith in our fans. Let's see what their response is. We'll talk about it in the morning. I'm exhausted. It's almost midnight."

"Ok, good."

Switching of the work light, CC climbed into one of the double beds. Anne lay on top of hers, staring at the cottage cheese ceiling. "Cottage cheese," she whispered. "I need to be working on my diet." She thought about Gladys. All alone, childless. What was her life? Did she have her own Nigel that she let go? Did she go down the road less traveled by, only to find a dead end? Was it a lonely walk? Anne held back the tears. This wasn't about her. This was about Gladys and the thousands of women like Gladys who felt without a purpose. There was nothing sadder in life than waking up every day with no purpose. No, this was not about Anne. Anne had a purpose, finding homes for orphaned artifacts, and Gladys was an orphaned artifact.

To the Rescue, Spoon Sisters blog

*D*EAR FRIENDS,
   As I sit reading the comments below, I am deeply moved by your generosity. With so much division in the country and in the world, it warms my heart to see strangers embrace a cause. I'm overwhelmed by the response, the call to action. It's reignited my fire. I've been focusing too much of late on the negative, the tragedy of Lindsey Kelly's passing. You, dear friends, have inspired me, rejuvenated me to continue our mission to help others, not just by finding lost treasures but to righting wrongs and discovering truths.

CC sat back and sipped her coffee. Fate had once again brought a mystery to their doorstep; it was up to them to solve it. She continued typing.

Anne and I will relay your offers to Gladys after we pay our final respects to Lindsey Kelly.

Hearing a stirring in the bed next to hers, CC spoke out loud, "Anne, take a look, you're not going to believe this." The glow of the PowerBook illuminated CC's face.

Anne rubbed her eyes. "What time is it?"

"5:20."

Stretching, Anne yawned. "What are you doing up so early?"

"Couldn't sleep. I've been thinking about Gladys all night. Come here. Take a

look."

She threw off the blanket and shuffled over to look over CC's shoulder. "What is this?"

"Responses from our fans. There has to be forty, maybe fifty, fans that want to help Gladys. Most of them live no more than a hundred miles from here."

"Really?"

"Joyce, she lives in Peoria. She says she is big fan of the Spoon Sisters." CC pointed to the comment and read out loud, "'I don't know if you remember, but you helped me find a Dale Earnhardt autographed fire suit for my husband, the NASCAR fan. I told him about Gladys. He was so grateful to you that he wants to help. We both want to help. I started a GoFundMe page for Gladys, and here's the link.' Another one writes, 'My husband is a real estate broker and owns property in Bloomington. He can find a commercial property for a reading center,'" CC read. "Here's a message from Ashley who lives in Washington, Illinois. 'I have plenty of books to donate. I'm a retired English teacher with free time.'" CC sipped her coffee, and sat back in the hard wooden chair. "The list goes on and on. I'm always amazed at the generosity of our fans."

Anne pulled up a chair and sat next to CC. "That's great. We should go tell Gladys."

"It's a little early."

After breakfast, the girls headed over to the former school now antique store. Passing through the booths to the gymnasium, Anne spotted a few things she hadn't seen the day before. Gathering the pen knife and the marble coasters into her arms, she found her friend inside the gym. Gladys was setting up her display. Anne was bursting with the news. She couldn't hold back. "Gladys, we have the best news ever."

Gladys pulled her horn-rimmed glasses off her nose and let them dangle from the chain around her neck. "Anne, what are you talking about?"

"CC wrote about you last night. Thousands of our fans want to help you build a resource center. All the details aren't clear yet, but there's lot of people who want to help with money, books, and their time."

Gladys pulled up a folding chair and sat down. "I don't understand. How did this all happen?"

"It's the power of the blog. These are all good people. They appreciate what you want to do, and they want to help."

"Anne, slow down," CC said. "You're overwhelming her."

Gladys interrupted. "What do I do? How do I talk to these blog fans?"

Anne giggled. "Don't worry about that. CC and I will handle everything."

"I don't know what to say. This is wonderful."

Anne could see Gladys' eyes clear up a bit. She understood the feeling. She needed a purpose to wake up every morning. Gladys needed this purpose, and Anne needed to find it for her. Her new orphaned artifact friend Gladys would have a home.

"Gladys, we'll work out all the details. We'll keep in touch. Unfortunately we're leaving today," CC interrupted. "For Springfield."

"Oh, I'm so sorry to hear that."

"We're going to see the exhibit of Civil War gowns at the Lincoln Museum."

"That's right. You have the Keckley dress," Gladys said, reaching under the table and pulling out a worn leather bound book. "I want to give you the book I wrote you about. It's the first printing of *30 Years a Slave* by Elizabeth Keckley."

"That has to be very valuable. I couldn't."

"No, I insist." Gladys handed the book to Anne. "I could never bring myself to sell any of my first editions. They're too precious to me, but knowing everything you've done for me, I want you to have it. I know it'd be in good hands."

"I understand. There are some things you can't sell. Only priceless treasures can be given." Anne placed her hand over Gladys, holding the book.

"I think you'll find it interesting reading. You know, Mrs. Lincoln put pressure on the publishers to pull the first printing of the book, so there are very few remaining. Mrs. Lincoln felt Mrs. Keckley divulged too much privileged information."

"I can't wait to read it. I'm so excited." Anne hugged Gladys and carefully tucked the slim volume in her bag.

RIP, Lindsey Kelly, Spoon Sisters Blog

*D*EAR FRIENDS,
Today Anne and I are attending Lindsey Kelly's funeral. Even though we only met her once, we felt we should pay our respects. Her journey to see Anne's dress being her final destination.

Gladys is overwhelmed by the response to help with the reading resource center. She will be in contact with those of you who live in the area. Anne and I are available to help as needed. We are thrilled at the response and hope to meet you all in person at the grand opening.

CC glanced down at a comment from Dr. Smart whose address showed as Michigan.

"Dear CC, I read your blog about Ms. Kelly and her fatal allergic reaction. If she did die from anaphylaxis shock, she most likely would have a history of severe allergic reactions. She should have been carrying an EpiPen, but you did not mention anything about it. I'm sure the police have looked into this, but I thought it worth mentioning. I'm an avid fan and somewhat of an amateur sleuth myself." CC scratched the back of her neck. She felt imaginary hives and cleared her throat.

She returned to her typing.

We continue our search for items on our request list. We hope to be checking them off on this trip. But for now, dear friends, toodooloo.

As CC posted the blog, she could see Anne studying her reflection in the mirror. She was glad she had brought her best vintage Dior black day dress. It had been quite a find hidden deep in a closet at an estate sale. "Are you ready?" CC asked, more practically garbed in dress pants and a blouse.

Streams of people flowed up the steps of the funeral home. "Is that?" Anne asked, pointing to the glamorous Kate Sparrow, star of stage and screen.

Eyeing the growing crowd in the funeral parlor, CC recognized several stars of ascending fame.

"Oh my goodness, look. It's Angela. I can't believe it," Anne said, making a move toward the elegant elderly actress.

"Sssh, don't bother her. This isn't the place." CC grabbed Anne's arm.

"It was my favorite show growing up. I've watched every episode. In fact, more than once. I aspire to be her. I have to at least say hi." Anne pulled away.

Before CC could stop her, Anne sat down next to the actress. "Excuse me, Miss Lans..."

"You can call me Angela."

"Really, Angela? I had to say I'm such a big fan. Murder." Someone ssshd Anne from behind.

"Dear, thank you so much," she whispered.

"How did you know Lindsey?" Anne whispered back.

"She helped find a dress for a movie I was shooting. A period piece."

"I just loved *Bedknobs. . .*"

Another shh came from behind but still Anne couldn't contain her enthusiasm. "You know, Miss Lans... I mean Angela, I'm a bit of a detective myself. More in the field of antiques. I'd love to get your perspective about a case I'm on right now."

"Oh, dear, that was just a character."

"Yes, of course, I understand. You played an amateur sleuth, an ordinary woman thrust into extraordinary situations. That's me!"

This time Anne felt a hand on her shoulder. She looked up. It was the Clark Gable doppelganger, Cliff Landry. He bent down and whispered in her ear. He smelled wonderful. "Can you please hold it down? The service is starting," he said. "Do you want to pay your respects?"

Anne nodded, then rose and approached the deceased. An open casket was something she dreaded, bringing back memories of her lost parents and her Great-Aunt Sybil. She stared down at Lindsey who stared back up at her. The embalmer had done a wonderful job; she looked beautiful. She wore a Kelly green St. John suit from this year's collection. There was no sign of swelling around her neck, which was accented by a green paisley printed Hermes scarf. Anne pondered about the fortune she must have spent on scarves, but Lindsey wore them well in life and in death.

CC stood next to Anne and mouthed a silent prayer. Anne whispered, "Can we go? I'm not feeling very well."

"Of course."

Anne Hillstrom, Spoon Sisters Blog

"*D*EAR FRIENDS,
    I'm writing as we drive down I-55 headed to Spring-field. CC asked me to update you all," Anne read aloud as she typed. "*I do have to say CC has been very gracious allowing me to write some of her blogs. I've noticed a change in her as of late. I can see why she enjoys writing this blog. It's very cathartic. I feel I can tell you, our fans, all my deepest secrets. One secret I will reveal is that I went off my diet today. You might imagine how upsetting it was attending Lindsey Kelly's service. I might have had one or two or more cookies with my tea. Lindsey appeared at peace. Many stars attended the service because Lindsey and her sister helped find period dresses for movies and TV shows. Just to reveal one more little secret, I sat next to a hero of mine. CC doesn't want me to mention who, but I will drop a hint. She played a murder mystery writer and an amateur sleuth, just like me, oh, and CC. She was most delightful.*

    I did not have the opportunity for much shopping in Bloom-ington, but I assure you I will more than make up for it in Spring-field. As many of you know, I occasionally write the Anne Hill-strom, Antique Hunters tip of the day. Today in honor of Lindsey, I will share how to tell an authentic vintage clothing item from a fake. First, observe the detail and the quality as they are the biggest clues, followed by the tag which will tell you everything. If an item has a union label, you can be sure it is vintage and made in the United States. Then check the fabric. Vintage items do not contain spandex. They should be one hundred percent cot-

ton, silk, rayon, polyester or wool. Also some people have been known to put a vintage designer tag on a fake dress so check to see if the tag is loose or sewn sloppily. Stitching should be done by hand and the item should be fully lined. Until later, happy shopping!"

Closing the iPad lid, Anne pulled out the Keckley book. She flipped through the brittle pages of the old book as the Illinois flatland drifted by in a blur of beige. Anne drifted in and out of consciousness. The hum of the motor, the stark landscape, the lack of sleep—her eyes closed slowly until there were only pinholes of light, and then she heard the war drums. She dreamed of the night she met John Blackbear, chief of the North Carolina Cherokee. His raven black hair and obsidian eyes, his broad shoulders and barrel chest, his gentle touch. She and CC had been stranded in the Smoky Mountains, and he had rescued them. He had also rescued Anne from a life of loneliness. The relationship had ended, but his memories lingered.

"Anne, are you ok?"

"What, what'd you say?"

CC glanced over from the driver's side. "You were moaning in your sleep."

"Oh."

"You said something about drums."

Anne shook her head, shaking off the memory. "No, no I didn't. I... I...found something really interesting in this first edition." She flipped the pages back. "Elizabeth Keckley started a school for runaway slaves in Washington D.C., but she writes that there were many opposed to it."

"Fascinating. Yes, during the Civil War even in some northern states, it was against the law to teach slaves to read. D.C. would have been right on the border."

" That might be why Mary Todd put a kibosh on the first edition," Anne continued. "The book also contains a lot of gossip about Mary Todd and her episodes—spells, as she calls them."

"Is there anything about Isobel Grant or the dress?"

"No, nothing so far. Do you think she's related to General Grant?" Anne said.

"I did a search on Isobel Grant and nothing came up. There are no records of General Grant having any relations with the name Isobel. His wife's name was Julia."

Anne screamed. "Stop."

CC slammed on the brakes, the VW slid into the shoulder narrowly missing the guardrail. "What? What is it?"

"You didn't see the billboard?" Anne craned her neck as if she could read the sign from behind. "Lincoln Highway Antiques."

"What are you talking about?"

"The billboard back there. Lincoln Highway Antiques ten miles." Anne clicked on her iPhone. "They're open til nine. They've got some great things. A lot of primitives, a lot of locally made Amish furniture, and other fine collectibles. We have to stop."

CC let out an audible sigh. "Don't ever yell stop like that when I'm driving. I thought I was about to hit a deer or something." She checked her watch. "It's almost five. We can catch a couple hours at the antique store."

"That's a great idea." As Anne scrolled through the pictures of antiques, she saw early Native American arrowheads, and the war drums started in her head again.

They curved off the exit ramp. The antique mall was directly to the right. CC pulled into the gravel parking lot, which had four loading docks. "Looks like an old factory," she said.

Anne read out loud. "In 1930, it was a Mason jar factory."

"Interesting," CC said, admiring the pile of wrought iron gates that leaned against the building.

Anne passed by her, flying inside. She breathed in the must and memories. It was one of her favorite fragrances. She gazed down the rows and rows of dusty shelves, rusty relics, orphaned artifacts. CC tapped her on the shoulder. "Let's check our fan list. If we're going to walk around, might as well make the most of our visit here."

"Yes, yes, of course, fan list," Anne said, barely acknowledging her friend.

A young girl sat on a tall metal stool behind a raised desk. She appeared to be the only one in the store and was thoroughly engrossed in her phone. She gave them a disinterested gaze. "Are you looking for something in particular, ladies?"

"We're just browsing," Anne said.

"We're closing early tonight. My boss went home sick." Her attention returned to her phone.

"Thank you," CC said as Anne rushed past her.

She was already halfway down the first aisle, picking up vases, putting them back down, flipping over china plates. "The list," CC said, catching up from behind. Anne hmmphed, reached into her bag to retrieve her iPhone. She checked the time. "The store is closing in two hours. Why don't we split up? We can cover more ground. Cindy Agin from Morton Grove, she's a longtime fan, is searching for an antique armoire or chifferobe, but she wants something different. I'll head upstairs."

Climbing the stairs, she stopped to catch her breath on the landing. She thought about the treadmill she had dragged to the garage from her old house. It was the most exercise she had gotten from it. Now the treadmill and her old house were gone, stuck in limbo. She could neither build nor sell. All that remained were the remnants of an ancient Indian burial ground and a mile of red tape. Never mind. She loved her cozy apartment above the store. Let the lawyers and the city battle it out. She would be fine.

She finally reached the second floor and sat down on a Victorian horsehair chair. Mothers had used this uncomfortable fabric to stop suitors from overstaying their welcome. Anne wiggled her butt along the rough fabric. Yes, this would have done the trick all right, jumping out of the chair. She ran her finger along a Chippendale coffee table, picturing it in her small living room. She would have to move out her existing table to make it fit. She wandered along the uneven rows of furniture, stopping to admire the Bakelite handles on a dresser, all original. A gilt mirror beckoned. She stared at her reflection, her blonde hair shining under the fluorescent lights. Plucking one gray hair out, she stared at it. Then she twisted and turned, admiring her figure. The endless diets had worked. She had whittled off the ten pounds she gained after Nigel had left. Her 40-something birthday was approaching even though she felt more 20-something. A benefit of her Swedish genes. Her Great-Aunt Sybil was beautiful at age 75, not a wrinkle and nary a worry. Anne's blonde hair now washed in golden sunlight from the skylight. She pulled another gray hair out. "That's two. This is something new," she said out loud. No one heard her. The upstairs was empty. Hearing CC's sensible clogs clicking up the stairs, she checked the time on her phone.

"There you are, Annie," CC said. "Are you ready to go? I'm getting tired."

"The store's open for another hour," Anne protested.

"I'm tired."

"Why don't you go to the room? Settle in. I'll call you when I'm done," Anne said.

"Ok." CC went back down the stairs.

Anne continued her search. Then she found it. She had been looking for such a piece her entire life. She had searched Chicago, she had searched Paris, but she never expected to find it here, buried in this building in downstate Illinois. She touched the wood with a reverence. It was a gorgeous enormous three-door armoire cabinet with deep walnut exterior and inlaid floral design. Stepping around to the back, she saw it, his signature, the famous artist Louis Majorelle, one of the founders of the French Art Nouveau movement. Anne had only seen his craftsmanship in books, never in person. This actually took her breath away. It was stunning, a major work of art. She took a step back to study it. and then opened the doors. She thought about one of the favorite childhood books, *The Lion, the Witch and the Wardrobe*. She stepped inside and closed the doors, expecting to open them and be transported to Narnia. Instead she felt herself falling. The armoire crashed on top of her, pinning her to the cement floor. Her head bounced with a crack. She saw stars and then she saw Narnia. The lion spoke with a British accent. He was wearing a bowler and his face morphed into that of the very tall and very British Nigel Towers, her beloved. "Annie, so glad you came to visit. I've missed you."

"Nigel, is that you?"

"Yes, Annie, welcome to my kingdom."

Around her the beavers who had CC's and Ingrid's faces darted about. Anne ran to embrace Nigel, hugging his mane. A carriage pulled by periwinkle blue horses thundered in, the ground shook, and the witch Betsy Buttersworth stepped out of the carriage. She was wearing a long, flowing periwinkle blue robe. "How dare you embrace my lion!" She pointed a blue wand at Anne.

Anne sucked in the oxygen, and then pulled the mask off her face. The EMT forced it back over her nose and mouth. "What's going on?" she mumbled.

CC bent down next to her. "Anne, you have a concussion. The girl from the store found you."

"Where am I?"

"You're in the emergency room at Springfield General Hospital."

She sat up on the gurney and looked around. "Where's Nigel? "What are you talking about?" CC asked.

"What happened?" Anne shook off her vision of Nigel.

"An armoire fell on top of you."

Anne recalled the armoire, its elegance, its historic importance. What a tragedy if it was lost. "Is it OK?" Anne asked

CC shook her head. "You were nearly crushed to death."

"Is it ok?" Anne repeated.

"For the most part it's fine. The one door was scratched up."

"How'd it fall over? It has to weigh 600 pounds."

CC shook her head.

"I climbed inside to get a better look," Anne said. "I must have tipped it over. Can we go? I'm fine."

"They want to keep you overnight to keep an eye on you. You have a slight concussion."

"I feel fine."

"I could stay with you."

Anne reached for a cup of water with a shaking hand. "No, I think I need to get some rest. Why don't you go back to the hotel? I'll see you in the morning."

CC squeezed Anne's hand, gazing up at the night nurse who had walked into the room. At the look of concern on CC's face, the nurse said, "She'll be fine. We'll take good care of her."

CC smiled and left Anne but stopped into a nearby waiting room to work.

Just a Bump, Spoon Sisters Blog

*D*EAR FRIENDS,
   I sit here writing to you from Springfield General Hospital. Don't worry, it's just a bump. Anne had a run in with an antique armoire. They are keeping her overnight for observation, but she seems fine. In case there was something on the news about the incident, she wanted you— her fans, our fans—to be the first to know that she is ok.

CC smiled, thinking of how Anne believed everything she did was of major importance.

And, furthermore, she wanted you to know that the armoire is safe and survived the ordeal. She requested I post pictures of it and contact Cindy Agin in particular. That's our Annie, always on the hunt.

CC noticed another comment from Dr. Smart. "Dear CC, I've contacted a friend of mine, a pathologist who works with the Chicago Police. There were no signs of epinephrine in her system. I thought you should know."

She continued typing.

The hour is late. I must cut this blog short. Until next time, dear friends, toodooloo.

After checking one last time on Anne, CC headed out to the hotel.

The red neon vacancy sign flickering at the Lincoln Inn went dark. CC drove up to the front of her room at the low two-story building. Each room had its own door facing the parking lot. "It's just for the night," she mumbled. She struggled with the key, looking up and down the walkway. It was nearly midnight; most of the rooms were dark. Taking a deep breath, she opened the door. She was greeted by burnt orange carpet, complete with coffee stains and cigarette burns. The scratchy mud brown cotton duvet was not in much better condition. She peeled it back with one eye closed, waiting to see what was underneath. At least the blanket appeared to be reasonably clean. She sat on the edge, settling into the lump, staring up at the painting over the bed depicting the landscape of a place she would never want to visit.

She longed for a stiff drink and a cigarette. Neither one was handy. Walking to the window, she peeked out through the curtains. The highway that ran along the parking lot was empty; there was no traffic. There were only four other cars in the lot. She glanced up at the hill adjacent to the small motel, expecting to see Mrs. Bates gazing out the window of her Victorian house. Thankfully there was nothing there. In the VW bus she had left all their possessions. She was too tired to go back out and carry everything in.

"Ok, CC, you're letting your imagination get away from you. It's been a long day. I have to get some sleep." She clasped the curtains shut with a whoosh, disturbing years of dust and a moth. She kicked off her Dansk clogs, not wanting to remove anything else. For a moment she thought about updating her blog but was too tired to string words together. She climbed into bed with all her clothes on and flicked off the bedside table light.

The closed-in smell of the room made her feel claustrophobic, but she was too nervous to leave a window open. She lay still inside her coffin, staring up at the ceiling, counting the cracks. "Go to sleep," she said out loud. "Go to sleep." Something more than her surroundings was bothering her. The store girl said it took three EMTs to lift the armoire off Anne. There was no way Anne had caused it to tip. "What's that?" she said out loud, sitting up straight. She pulled the blanket around her.

"Was that the door? Did I hear the door? Was the door knob twisting?" It wouldn't take much for the lock to snap, and the chain on the door was more of an annoyance than a failsafe. She held her breath. The curtains lit up blood red as the vacancy sign hummed to life. Someone walked past the window, a shape, a shadow. She felt the urgency to run and fling open the door. Instead she ran and grabbed the small wooden chair by the work desk and jammed it under the door handle. She opened the edge of the curtain just a sliver. The walkway was empty. Just one cigarette, she thought.

It was a habit that had been hard to break. She had started smoking a year after she married her now ex-husband John Reeney. That was a nasty habit also. She checked her watch. It had only been ten minutes. "How can that be?" she thought. She sat on the edge of the bed. "No, Anne did not tip that armoire, and I know I heard the door knob twist."

Anne's Release, Spoon Sisters Blog

*D*EAR FRIENDS,
After a restless night at my hotel room, I am back at the hospital waiting to pick up Anne. If she is up to it, we will continue our plans to visit the Lincoln Museum. Being unable to sleep last night, I Googled some interesting information about the museum to share it with you. Built in 2005, it is the largest presidential museum in the country. Its 50,000 square feet are filled with immersion exhibits, a special effects theater, and original artifacts. It is a walkthrough experience in two parts – the first part about Mr. Lincoln's pre-presidential years and the second about the White House years. I am very excited to experience this historic monument.

Rather than designing the exterior first as is normal, the visitor experience was designed first by Imagination Arts. Then the architecture was built around the exhibits. Special effects from Hollywood and Broadway were used with the Illinois Historic Preservation Agency ensuring its accuracy. But don't mention the agency to Anne – she hasn't quite forgiven them for their stance on her house. I will give you an update on her house later, dear friends. Until later, toodooloo.

She sipped her Starbuck's Grande Americano. Mention of Anne's house made her think about hers and the need to cultivate her garden for summer planting. This year she would plant her hot pepper garden. She reached inside her bag and pulled out the small vial of ghost pepper powder she carried everywhere. It had become more than just a seasoning; it had saved her life several times. As she put the vial back in her purse, she felt her phone vibrate. Her boyfriend Nick's photo appeared. "Nick, how are you?" she asked.

"Hi CC, I was worried about you. I haven't heard from you other than the blogs. Is Anne ok?"

"Yes, I'm picking her up right now from the hospital. I've missed you. How are things at the station?"

"Good. Adam's been asking about Ingrid. He stopped over at the store a couple times to check on her."

"That's good. She's been busy between school and work."

"Listen, I wanted to talk to you about something. I was going to wait until you got back." There was silence.

"What's up, Nick?"

Nick cleared his throat. "Maybe we should talk when you get back."

"Now you have me curious."

"It can wait. I'm missing you too."

CC smiled, thinking of smoke and musk. "Nick, I've got to go. They're bringing Anne out."

"Oh, ok," he stuttered. "We'll talk soon. Bye."

CC shoved the phone back in her purse as the morning nurse wheeled Anne from around the corner. CC hugged her, bending over the wheelchair. "How do you feel?"

"I feel fine. As good as new. Let's get out of here." Anne stood up. Thanking the nurse, she followed CC out to the VW. "Can we stop for breakfast before we go to the museum? I'm starving."

CC took a sip of her coffee, nodding. She was distracted, her mind on Nick and his unasked question. They climbed in the VW and headed back to the highway toward downtown Springfield.

"So how was your night?" Anne asked.

"My back is killing me. Not a very comfortable bed."

"I had a premonition. Nigel came to me. He was a king, and he asked me to be his queen."

"You were knocked out cold."

"It seemed real. "

"When was the last time you heard from Nigel?"

"It's been six months. Not a letter, not a text. He came to the store that night and said there was a family emergency, and he was leaving for England. That's all he said."

"You were pretty tough on him. You know he was in love with

you."

"I love him, too, in my own way. I just wasn't ready for that type of permanent commitment." Anne rubbed the knot on the back of her head. She clicked on her iPhone and typed in Springfield breakfast. "Found it. Annabelle's."

"What?" CC glanced sideways. "What are you talking about?"

"Annabelle's. They make fresh biscuits slathered with locally sourced jams." She put the address in her GPS and directed CC to the small parking lot adjacent to a red brick doctor's office off the main campus of Sangamon University. The small parking lot was crowded with expensive SUVs. Anne jumped out of the bus as CC turned off the engine.

She peeked in the window of the small café which had a cozy, homey feel. Tables with terrarium tops filled with plants and rocks, multicolored chairs sat on by a mixture of tourists and twenty-something students. Anne could smell the biscuits and fresh ground coffee. Suddenly her head didn't ache but her stomach growled. The rosy-cheeked college girl behind the counter welcomed them with a big Midwest smile. "Can I help you?"

Anne ordered a biscuit with country ham, eggs, and gravy. CC lingered over the menu, finally choosing a scrambled egg and biscuit. They found a table in the corner, one of maybe ten. The room was comfortably crowded and lively with conversation. The couple at the table next to them proudly displayed their Chicago Cub T-shirts. CC felt right at home. Anne filled paper cups with the variety of jams from the side table—blackberry, lingonberry, boysenberry, strawberry. She ran the gamut of berries. The waitress brought over their plates. One entire plate was dedicated to the biscuit of Annabelle's fame. Anne slathered butter and jam on hers and took a healthy bite. "Mmm," she said, her mouth full. "This is so good." She thought about asking the waitress the nutritional values of the biscuit, but she imagined the carb count to be the upper five hundreds. No point unleashing that kind of trouble. Sometimes ignorance is bliss, especially when it comes to carbs. She took the last piece of biscuit and sopped up the remaining gravy.

After one bite, CC had headed back to the kitchen. She was determined to get the recipe for the biscuits. White and fluffy, crispy. She thought about the Bee's Knees Café. What a perfect biscuit to serve with their organic honey. In the six months since they had taken over managing the honey farm and café, business had doubled. Ingrid had her hands full. Thankfully she had Dakota and her mother helping out.

CC stuck her head into the small kitchen doorway. "Excuse me," she said. The large woman wearing a hairnet and apron that strained at the strings turned slowly. A woman of some years and size—exactly the appropriate image for a woman who could bake such a decadent biscuit.

"May I help you?" she asked with an accent as sweet as the butter she melted in the pan.

"I'm so sorry to disturb you. I had to stop and say how wonderful your biscuits are."

"Well, thank you, honey." She wiped the flour off her hands with a rag and took CC's hand in hers. "My name is Annabelle. This is my place."

"I'm CC Muller. I run a small café back in the Chicago area."

"How wonderful. We get a lot of folks from Chicago."

"I write a blog and like to share recipes with my fans. Would you be willing to share your biscuit recipe?"

"Oh, I'm sorry. I can't give that out. You understand, don't you?"

"Of course. I didn't think it would hurt to ask."

"I can share my honey butter recipe with you."

CC watched Annabelle as she mixed fresh unsalted butter with organic honey and then added a dash of her secret ingredient, a slight dab of chili paste. "Oh, wait," CC reached into her purse and pulled out a small vial.

"What's that, dear?"

"It's ghost pepper from my garden." CC unscrewed the tiny lid.

Annabelle took a sniff. "My goodness. That will wake you up, won't it? Shall we try just a little dab?" Annabelle took a pinch and added it to the mixture.

"You know," CC said, "if you like kicking it up a little, I have a recipe that I use at Sunday brunch back at the café."

Annabelle smiled, reached over and grabbed an apron, and

tied it around CC's waist.

"It's a frittata but with a little kick." CC scampered around the small kitchen, gathered onions, mushrooms, cream, cheddar cheese and poured them all into an iron skillet. She beat the eggs into the mixture and added three pinches of her ghost pepper powder. "We bake at 350 for 30 minutes. The trick is to cut the eggs up and serve them on one of your biscuits with a little dab of honey butter on top."

Annabelle grinned a big southern grin. "That sounds delicious, dear. We're going to call that the CC special." She gave CC a hug.

CC went outside where Anne was waiting not so patiently. "We have so much to do. According to the guidebook, there's an antique store on Main Street, Lincoln's birthplace, and an old candy store. And then if you drive a little ways out of—"

"We're here to find out more information about the dress. I think our first stop should be the museum. Toby contacted Rachel, the curator, and she is going to meet with us."

While Anne's visions of shopping flew out of her head, she pictured the dress. Her step quickened in her urgency to reach the car, and she jumped in. She put the address in her phone so she could direct CC to their destination. When they arrived they were greeted by rows of colorful tulips leading up to the museum.

CC parked in the adjacent parking lot. Lilacs released their delicious fragrance as fat bumblebees buzzed about. CC thought about Bandit. English ivy climbed the back walls of the limestone building.

Anne thought about Nigel and his kingdom.

They walked up the limestone stairs, entering the rotunda. Marble floors clicked under their heels. Abraham Lincoln's entire life passed before them. From his humble beginnings in a log cabin studying by candlelight, to his early career as a lawyer in Springfield. Mannequin replicas of young Lincoln greeted them at each exhibit, walking them through his life leading to his war room in the White House discussing the Emancipation Proclamation with his cabinet. Mary Todd knelt over the bed of her sick son. Mary and Abraham, arm in arm, sitting in the Presidential Box at Ford's Theater. His enshrined death mask. Anne stopped to admire the lifelike Mary Todd wearing a practical day dress and bonnet, wool and silk, very fashionable.

CC stopped and read the plaque in front of the display. It read, "Elizabeth Keckley, original." Anne felt a shiver down her spine, a connection to the past, an answer to the future.

CC whispered, "Rachel Contraldes. She's expecting us." They walked down the long hallway to the museum offices until they reached the door that had a sign above it, reading, "Curator." CC knocked gently.

A woman about their age answered the door. Her long black hair was a contrast to her pale white skin. Her brown eyes sparkled with welcome. "You must be CC Muller," she said with a warm smile and outreached hand.

CC shook her hand. "This is my partner, Anne Hillstrom."

"Of course. Please come in. Toby told me to expect you." She went back to a desk and pointed to two chairs that were facing it. Anne sank into one.

Rachel continued, "How do you know Toby? He didn't share any details with me."

"We were colleagues at one time at a small newspaper after college." CC shifted in her seat. "Toby has written many kind stories about our museum and has become a friend."

CC cleared her throat. "He may or may not have told you about why we are here today."

"Yes, he mentioned something about a Keckley dress, but I can't imagine you have an original. There are only a few known examples left of her work. And the Met snapped those up. Mrs. Lincoln sold off many of her possessions after President Lincoln was killed."

"I believe it is original." Anne opened the garment bag and pulled out the dress.

Rachel ran her fingers through the blue silk and checked the hem. "The material is correct for the era." She then turned it around and examined the hand-sewn label. "It appears to be Elizabeth Keckley's handiwork. Similar labels were found in Mrs. Lincoln's dresses. I'm not sure who Isobel Grant is." Rachel pondered the name. "As you can imagine, I've spent considerable time researching Mrs. Lincoln and the women who surrounded her in Washington, and I don't recall an Isobel Grant. Of course, there was Julia Grant, but she was…"

"Married to Ulysses S. Grant," CC interrupted, anxious to share her knowledge.

"Yes, she was married to General Grant, and she was included in Mrs. Lincoln's inner circle. Of course, they were rivals," Rachel said, pausing to run her fingers along the black beads that decorated the bodice of the dress. "These appear to be jet or perhaps glass. If this is an original Keckley, she would have used jet, which was more valuable. Either way this dress was made for a woman of means. But I've never seen this pattern before. It's very unusual. Once the war started, Mrs. Lincoln was asked to tone down her appearance in sympathy for those on the fighting lines. She gave up her frivolous ball gowns and dressed in more somber tones. If Isobel Grant was in her inner circle, she would have followed Mary Todd's example. The elaborate beadwork makes me think Isobel was not in Mary Todd's circle of friends. Keckley did create dresses for many Washington socialites on both sides. Either way this dress is quite valuable, no matter who wore it, and I would love to add it to our collection."

"We wanted to see the dresses you have on display to compare the workmanship," Anne said.

"All our dresses are reproductions. The woman who could have helped you is no longer with us."

"Lindsey," Anne said.

Rachel appeared shocked. "Lindsey. How did you know? Toby did not mention that you knew her."

"She came to see us about the dress. We actually found her." Anne paused. "She…" She paused again. "She came to our auction in Hampshire, but we didn't have the dress there. We brought the dress to her hotel room, and that's when we found her. She never got to see the dress."

Rachel sank down in her chair. "Oh my goodness, that's horrifying."

"Yes, it was."

"Lindsey never told me about this dress. She said she was leaving for a few days to visit her sister," Rachel said.

"Is there anyone else who would have known about the dress other than Lindsey?" CC asked.

"She kept to herself for the most part."

"How did you meet her?"

"I actually visited her dress store when I was doing research for the museum. She was an expert on dresses from the Civil War era. I was the one who offered her the position here." Rachel became quiet thinking about Lindsey.

Anne walked around the back of the desk and put her hand on her shoulder. "Could you help us find the provenance for this dress? The only information that we have is that it was owned by Sharon Prima. We weren't able to find any living relatives or much background about her."

"That's something I can help with. I have copied some extensive records on Civil War families from the Met in my private collection. Why don't you come over tonight for dinner, and we can go through my books?"

After arranging a time, CC and Anne left Rachel's office. They wandered around the museum, staring at the reproduction dresses. Anne pictured herself among the Washington socialites dancing at the president's inauguration ball with a very tall and very British General Nigel Towers. She imagined strolling onto the veranda in the moonlight while the strains of a Mozart waltz followed behind them, gazing at Nigel's dark eyes and pointy chin, feeling his bony chest against hers, and kissing his lips. She pulled out her iPhone and tried his number. It went to a fast busy signal. She put her phone away, grabbed CC by the arm. "Let's go to the hotel room. I have an idea."

Following the Dress, Spoon Sisters Blog

*D*EAR FRIENDS,

I have to say the Lincoln Museum exceeded my expectations. The craftsmanship and the detail—how amazing. I felt as if I were living history. We met with the curator, Rachel Contraldes, a lovely woman. Her extensive knowledge of Civil War-era fashions exceeded Anne's. She will help us authenticate Anne's dress. I must recommend if you are in the area that you stop in the museum and touch history, especially in our current political climate. It really resonates today.

We also enjoyed a lovely breakfast at Annabelle's. While she wouldn't share her biscuit recipe with me, she did share her honey butter recipe, which I now share with you, dear friends. Take 1 pound of butter, cut into chunks, put in mixing bowl, add ¼ cup honey, ½ teaspoon chili paste and if you are daring enough, ½ teaspoon ghost pepper powder. Mix together for 5 to 7 minutes. Place on parchment paper or plastic wrap and then roll into log. Chill for at least two hours. We will be serving this at our new Sunday brunch.

She glanced down and saw another comment from Dr. Smart, "Dear CC, I was rereading an old blog of yours about bee pheromone and allergic reactions to bee stings. I thought, what a clever murder plot."

CC felt a chill before returning to typing.

Until next time, dear friends, toodooloo.

She clicked on Google and searched "Dr. Smart, Michigan." Several doctors appeared, none of them allergists. Then she turned off her computer.

Not wanting to face another restless night, CC had upgraded

to the Doubletree in downtown Springfield. From their window, they could see the capitol building. She hadn't shared the reason for the switch with Anne, not wanting her to be nervous.

She jumped when the door opened, only to see that it was Anne, carrying the dress bag. "I went back to the car to get the dress," Anne said, as she took it out of the garment bag. "Give me a match."

"You're not going to set the dress on fire, are you?" CC asked.

"No, I want to test something." On the drive back to the hotel, Anne recalled some of her chemistry 101. The wasted years she had spent laboring as a research chemist at Ebbort Labs proved to be useful in her true calling as an antique hunter. She took her sewing kit out of her bag, then lit the needle with the match, holding it under one of the beads.

"What are you doing, Anne?"

Nothing happened. "I don't smell anything," Anne said. "If it was vulcanite, it would have an acrid smell." Anne then pulled her porcelain thimble out of her bag and ran one of the beads across it. It left a chocolate-colored streak on the thimble. "This is jet. This is an original Keckley. Someone making an imitation would not have used jet. It would have been too expensive."

CC checked her watch. "I'm sorry I have to go. I promised Toby I'd meet him for a drink."

"Toby, really?"

"He introduced us to Rachel. I think I owe him at least that, don't I?"

"That's fine. I'll check out a few of the shops in the area."

CC hurried into the bathroom. Minutes later, she came out wearing a flowered sundress. She had touched up her hair and makeup. Anne shook her head and sighed. "What? I can't look nice?" She grabbed her purse and left the room.

She drove slowly, looking left and right, searching for the pub. She forgot to mention to Nick she would be seeing an old boyfriend. Not really seeing, meeting. *That's a better way to put it.* Either way Toby was history and Nick was her future. She pulled up in front of the small galley pub decorated in dark wood and gold, named Barley's. It was relatively crowded for late afternoon and a little noisy. She had to adjust her eyes to the cool darkness.

The long, narrow room was dotted with bar-height tables and stools. The walls were decorated with autographed St. Louis Cardinals and Cubs memorabilia. *Might as well hedge your bet both ways.* It was relatively clean but nothing that extraordinary. It could be any bar, any town. CC recognized Toby right away. He was standing in the corner, speaking with a couple of patrons. When he saw her, he gave her a big smile. He had aged well, she thought. Still pretty fit. Never a dapper dresser, he was wearing a brown flannel shirt and faded jeans. His hair was a little grayer and thinner, but his brown eyes still had a bit of a sparkle. As he came up, he hugged her, and then he pulled back and kissed her on her cheek. "CC, you look great."

"Thanks, Toby."

"Should we sit down?" He led her over to the only corner booth. As the waitress came over, Toby looked at CC.

"I'll have a glass of red wine."

"I'll have the same, Nancy," Toby said.

"Toby, this place is very nice. How long have you owned it?"

"Actually, I'm part owner. Going on five years now."

"How do you manage running the bar and the paper?"

Toby shrugged. "You make time for what you love."

CC realized why they had never become more than a fling. She had already run out of conversation. The waitress brought over their wine. CC sipped it nervously. "I wanted to thank you for connecting me with Rachel and giving me the background info on Lindsey."

"How's that going for you?" Toby asked, finishing his glass and waving for another.

"Actually we're having dinner with Rachel tonight. I can't stay long." CC glanced at her watch.

Toby grabbed CC's hand. "Really? I thought we could make a night of it."

CC slowly pulled her hand back, putting it on her lap. "Did you find out anything else about Lindsey Kelly?"

"Before she moved to Bloomington, she and her sister lived in Batavia. That's not so far from where you're at, right?" Toby paused, waiting for her response. She nodded.

CC checked her watch again. "Toby, I don't mean to be rude,

but I don't want to be late for dinner. I wanted to thank you again." She stood up.

Toby squeezed out from behind the table to hug her. "You can stop here after dinner. I'm closing the bar tonight."

"Sure," CC said with an air of doubt. "Thank you, again." She kissed him on the cheek and hurried out of the bar.

Anne strolled along Main Street, darting from one shop to another, nibbling on a chocolate cream from Pease's Candy. She was in her element in this antique treasure trove of shops. She was mostly window shopping as her budget was slim. Intrigued by a dangling amethyst pendant, she entered a small storefront. After trying on the pendant and setting it aside, Anne wandered through the cluttered aisles. Glass shelves were brimming with picture frames, perfume bottles, and crystal candlesticks. She picked up a sterling silver picture frame, examining it before setting it back down.

She spotted an inkwell in the corner of a shelf. She reached for it, almost knocking over a Lalique figure. Its exterior was gold with maidenheads adorning it in a neoclassical design. In the center the pen tray drifted like a lily pad toward the center-cut glass inkwell with its hinged ornate gilded lid. Its bottom was stamped "Elkington's Art Gold Bronze Registered." This would be perfect for Stanley, who had written her searching for an antique inkwell for his wife, who was a writer. She placed it with the pendant and then continued browsing, gliding through the narrow hallway into the back room. After paying for her purchases and arranging to have them delivered to the hotel, she went back out into the street.

Next door was Daisies' Boutique, advertising vintage dresses. A pansy festooned sundress, a close cousin to her beloved capri pants, beckoned her. "Oh my goodness, that's fate," she said. She rushed into the store to check the size. A hand reached past her to grab the dress. Anne smiled politely and grabbed it first. It was only slightly smaller than her current size. A week or two watching her weight, and the dress would fit perfectly.

The crowded store was buzzing with conversation, dresses flung off of racks, purses swinging back and forth. The sign over the cash register read, "One-day sale, 50 percent off." Anne's heart raced. "Miss, may I try this on? Do you have a room?" Anne interrupted the young store clerk who was wrapping packages. She waved to the back of the crowded store. Anne ran into a small fitting room, pulled the curtain closed, and slipped on the dress. Twirling about, she struggled to pull up the zipper. She sucked in all the air she could, admiring herself front and back. She realized there was no price tag, a prickly peccadillo.

Anne made her way to the front of the line. "Excuse me, miss, I have no idea whatsoever how much this dress costs."

The girl held up her finger and sshed Anne as she continued ringing up purchases. The line of women at the counter gave Anne a pointed look. Anne was reaching her limit. Patience was a virtue far down on her list of virtues. "Honey, you should buy that," a voice said from behind her.

She turned to see an elderly woman with several dresses folded over her arm. She had on a red fedora with a gold hatpin. "You think?"

"Definitely."

"Thank you. I'm Anne Hillstrom."

"I'm Catherine. "

"I love your hatpin."

The woman smiled, touching her antique gold bumblebee hatpin. "Thank you, honey. I collect antique hatpins."

"What a coincidence. I own an antique store. I'd love to talk to you about your collection. Let me give you my card." Anne reached to her side and realized her bag, the bag, was not with her. "Oh my goodness, please excuse me." She ran back to the dressing room. Anne could see a pair of large purple pumps, sticking out from under the curtain. She tapped on the wall. "Excuse me, I left my purse in there. It's orange, it's Prada, it's large."

The curtain swished open. "There's no purse in here."

Anne's heart skipped a beat. She stuck her head in the doorway. She ran back through the crowd, skipped the line and went right to the front of the counter. "Ma'am you're going to have to wait in line."

"You don't understand. My purse, my bag, it's gone. It's a large orange Prada. . ."

The girl squatted down, shuffling behind the counter, retrieved

Anne's bag, and placed it on the counter.

"Oh my goodness," Anne said, hugging her bag like a lost child.

"Somebody brought it up from the dressing room."

"Thank you so much." Anne grabbed the purse and turned to the door.

"Ma'am, ma'am," the girl called back after her.

Anne stopped in the doorway, glancing at the sundress she was still wearing. "I'm so sorry." She paid for the dress and wore it, carrying a bag with her clothes.

Then she continued on to the next store, an art gallery. Pictures and paintings lined the exposed brick wall, ascending sizes, colors, and shapes. She admired a frame. A young couple also stood staring at a painting depicting Lincoln's Gettysburg Address. The painting was marked $150. Anne carefully lifted the small painting off the wall and checked the back. It read, "Newcomb Macklin." She glanced at the young couple. "Are you interested in this painting?"

"Yes, we recently moved here and are renting our first apartment together."

Anne smiled before taking a deep breath.

"Why, were you going to buy it?" the young woman asked.

"Oh, no, but let me show you something." She turned the painting over again. "The frame is worth more than the painting. This mark Macklin means that it's a Newcomb Macklin, which was founded in 1871. It's the oldest, continuous running framing company in the United States. It's hand carved and gilded. It's worth over $1,000," she whispered.

"Really?" the young woman gasped. "Wow. We could resell it and buy some living room furniture. I'm sorry, ma'am, but I never asked your name."

Anne bristled at 'ma'am.' "Anne Hillstrom."

"You sure know a lot about picture frames."

"I'm an antique hunter." She reached into her purse and retrieved her business card embossed "Anne Hillstrom, Antique Hunter." "My partner and I write a blog about antiques, and we operate an antique store outside of Chicago. Let me show you a couple things." She turned the frame over. Anne was in her element. She loved lessons to others. "Here's how you can tell an antique frame from a fake. First the wood in the back should appear worn and aged. It should be dark and uneven and might even have a lighter area where a label was located and later removed. If the wood looks light or new, it's probably not an antique. Check for markings on the back. Pick up the frame and test the weight. Antique frames tend to be heavier than reproductions. Look for leaf lines. Gold and silver leaf come in thin sheets and are applied delicately. When the layers of leaf overlap, these are called leaf lines. Cheaper frames do not have leaf lines."

"Miss Hillstrom, this is fascinating."

"Please call me Anne."

"I'm Bobby and this is my husband, Brandon."

"Do you like antique hunting?"

"Very much so. My mother took me with her when I was little. She gave me many of her antiques when we got married." "I'll tell you what, Bobby, that's my email address. You send me a list of antiques you might be looking for, and I'll keep an eye open. Ok?"

"Thank you. I don't know what to say."

"To start, buy that painting and sell the frame." Anne winked. Like a superhero of antiques, she was gone onto the next shop. She felt like a superhero, swooping in and saving that young couple. Using her finely honed skills, she walked with more pep in her step, nibbling on her chocolate creams. She felt her iPhone vibrate, pulled it out of her bag, and sat on a bench outside the store. The caller ID read, Ingrid. "Hi, Ingrid." "Hi, Anne."

"I can barely hear you. Where are you?"

"I'm at the store. We have Dakota's kid's antique sale today. It's packed in here."

Anne could hear the loudest voice of all in the background, saying cupcakes. "Buttersworth," she muttered.

"Anne, how is it going with you? Any information on the dress?"

"I found out that the beading is jet, which leads me to believe it is an authentic Keckley. We're having dinner with the curator of the Lincoln Museum tonight."

"That's wonderful," she screamed over the little girl's squeals.

"Sounds like you're having fun there."

"The greatest time. Betsy brought all the girls to her sweet shop and let them decorate their own cupcakes."

"Yeah, that Buttersworth she's a pip. How are the cats?"

"That's one of the reasons I was calling. There's been a little bit of trouble. Do you remember that Phoenix vase you won in the box lot? The one on the mantle over the fireplace?"

Anne cringed, picturing the mint green vase adorned with Art Nouveau figures. "Yes, I love that vase."

"I found it in pieces on the floor. Somebody knocked it off the mantle."

Anne sighed.

"Sassy is not eating. She seems very troubled about your visitors."

"I keep a special can of her favorite treat hidden in the back of the pantry. You can give her a couple spoonsful on the blue Belleek plate. It's her favorite plate. Tell her I love her and I'll be home soon. Thank you so much for watching all of them."

"Of course, Anne. I've got to go," Ingrid said. Anne could hear a little girl asking Ingrid questions as the phone went dead.

Her iPhone pinged again. A text from CC. "Where are you? We're going to be late." Picking up her packages, Anne headed back to the hotel, never seeing the man who had been watching her.

CC was waiting in the lobby. "Where have you been?"

"Wandering around." Anne glanced in the full-length mirrors that hung on the lobby walls, admiring herself.

"Is that new?" CC asked.

"Do you like it?" Anne twirled around.

"We have to hurry," CC said, leading Anne out of the lobby to the VW. A short drive later, they arrived at a 1920s brown brick bungalow. It reminded Anne of the bungalow she had once owned. Rachel was sitting on her front porch swing and waved Anne and CC up the front steps. CC handed her a bottle of wine. "Thank you." Rachel stood up. "Come inside." She opened the front door, and they followed her into the small entryway. A large painting of a pear dominated the space.

The original 1920s oak chair rails and crown molding were polished to perfection. On either side of the brick fireplace were matching built-in bookcases cluttered with books. Anne felt sad, missing her bookcases, her books, and her bungalow. From the living room, they walked through an archway into a formal dining room with a beautiful crystal chandelier. Anne touched the crystals listening for the telltale ping while Rachel ran to the kitchen to open the wine. The chandelier was very fine, probably Schoenbeck. Rachel had wonderful taste.

The dining room table and chairs were also antiques, early 1940s, long cherry table with elaborately scrolled legs, high-backed chairs with cushions encased in a William Morris deep burgundy thistle fabric. Anne snuggled down in one. Rachel returned, carrying the open bottle and the wine glasses. She filled each one. "Cheers. Here's to new friends," she said, clinking their glasses.

Anne noticed the wedding band on her finger. "Your husband's not joining us?"

"He's away on business."

Anne looked around the cozy dining room. Family pictures covered an entire wall. One was of Rachel holding a beautiful green-eyed black cat. "Where's your kitty? I'd love to meet her."

Rachel sat down across from Anne at the table. "That's Shadow. She was about a year old in that picture. She passed just before Christmas last year."

"I'm so sorry."

"She was eighteen. She had a good life."

"She looks like Luna, Lindsey's cat."

"Yes, she does. I forgot about Luna and Reina. I went with Lindsey to the shelter when she adopted them. It was right after she moved here," Rachel said. "What happened to them?"

"I have them now," Anne said.

"Lindsey loved those two. I'm glad they're in good hands."

CC interrupted. "It smells really good."

"Thank you. I've made lasagna. It's an old family recipe." Rachel doled out the lasagna.

Anne bent her head down toward the plate and took a big whiff. Lots of gooey mozzarella, carbs be damned.

While they ate, CC asked, "How long have you been at the museum?"

"I've been there for ten years. Before that I was at the Met."

"Oh, I love the Met," Anne said, through a bite full of lasagna.

"When the Lincoln Museum was creating its dress collection, they offered me the job as curator." Rachel cleared the dishes. When she returned, she said, "I brought up all my boxes that I brought with me from the Met. I have copies of original letters from Mary Todd and newspaper articles from Washington during the Civil War. It was for my research when I was working on the exhibits. I thought maybe we could go through the boxes and see if we could find anything about the dress or Isobel Grant."

Rachel led them into the sunroom. On one wall, there was a large display case with antique wax seals. "My goodness, what a collection. You must have over a hundred," Anne said, studying them.

Rachel smiled. "I actually started my collection while I was in New York, and it keeps growing."

"May I?" Anne asked as she lifted up a seal. "Is that the Vanderbilt crest?"

"It's not his personal seal, but it was used by the head of his staff," Rachel said. "There's an interesting story about Vanderbilt's contribution to the Civil War."

CC interrupted. "Yes, of course. He loaned his steamship, the Vanderbilt, to the Union Army during the second year of the Civil War. A part of the Union blockade, she was outfitted with heavy guns and set out on the high seas to search for raiders from the Confederate States, which were inflicting damage to the Union commercial ships. President Lincoln proclaimed the blockade in April 1861 which monitored 3,500 miles, including New Orleans and Mobile."

"You do know your history," Rachel said. "Vanderbilt offered to help the Union at the outbreak of the Civil War. It wasn't until 1861 that Lincoln finally accepted his offer and gave him a million dollars to outfit his ship. I've made copies of some of the letters that were found after the war. Of course, in 1860 and 1861, Washington was cut off from the rest of the Union, so correspondence was difficult if not impossible. Confederates captured any messages coming out of the city."

"Here's a lovely one from 1930s." Anne looked up, having missed the entire conversation.

"I have a lot of Art Deco-era seals. That one belonged to Tallulah Bankhead. I have the matching melting spoon she used to melt the wax. I bought it at an estate sale when I was in Los Angeles."

As Anne continued to admire her seal collection, CC opened a box and sifted through papers. Two hours and three bottles of wine later, CC held up a piece of paper. "Rachel, this appears to be an invoice for pencils and paper and early readers."

"And?" Anne asked.

"And it's signed by Isobel Grant and paid for by Elizabeth Keckley," CC said. "I can't make out this seal, it's so faded." CC peered closely at the brittle paper.

Rachel took out a magnifying glass and studied the seal. "I can't make it out either," she said. "Let me do some research."

CC stumbled to the couch.

"Are you ok?" Rachel asked.

"A little too much wine. I got carried away."

Rachel glanced at Anne who was yawning. "I have plenty of room if you want to stay the night. I'd rather you didn't drive back to the hotel."

"We couldn't be an imposition."

"I'd enjoy the company."

Yawning, CC looked at Anne who nodded. "Wait," Anne said, running out to the VW, grabbing the dress, and running back in. "Now that I know it's real, I'm not letting it out of my sight."

CC thought about the twisting doorknob at the Lincoln Inn and nodded silently. They could never be too careful.

Waxing Poetic, Spoon Sisters Blog

DEAR FRIENDS,
      We had a lovely dinner with our new friend, Rachel, the curator of the Lincoln Museum. Rachel shared some of her historical knowledge about the Lincolns with Anne and myself. It appears that Anne's dress may indeed be an original Keckley.

Rachel also collects wax seals. I've uploaded several pictures of some of her collection, including ones that belonged to Commodore Vanderbilt and Tallulah Bankhead.

For those of you who did not attend, I'm glad to say that the children's antique sale at Great-Aunt Sybil's Attic was a great success. Ingrid and Dakota did a wonderful job and a special thank you to our dear friend Betsy Buttersworth for supplying the cupcakes.

"Buttersworth," Anne muttered in her sleep.

"Yes, Buttersworth," CC typed, smiling.

We're hot on the trail of the mysterious Isobel Grant. As you know, that name was sewn into the label of Anne's dress along with Keckley's. I feel the puzzle is coming together. We've started with the corner puzzle pieces as is best to do, and slowly we're filling in the center. I have to say I've enjoyed sharing each day's adventure with you, dear friends. I've made it a priority to stop whatever I'm doing to keep you updated. I feel like you're along for the ride, sitting in the back of the VW bus, peering over our shoulder, looking down the road as we embark on our biggest adventure yet. Until next time, dear friends, toodooloo.

CC rubbed her eyes and reached over the nightstand. She checked the time on her iPhone, glanced at Anne who was snoring softly from the other twin bed. Sitting on the edge of the bed, she stretched. She threw on her blouse. "Where'd I leave my jeans?" she asked out loud, dancing from one foot to the other. "I can't wait any longer." Opening the bedroom door, she checked the hallway. It was all clear. As she reached the bathroom door, it flew open. Behind it stood a handsome, dark-haired man wearing nothing but a smile. His short black hair dripped from the shower. CC gasped and pulled her short blouse towards her knees. "Excuse me?" she gasped.

The man reached behind him, grabbed a hand towel and attempted to ease CC's embarrassment. "I'm sorry. I got in late last night. Rachel was sleeping. I didn't know we had guests. I'm her husband, Jeremy."

Hunched over, CC smiled and waved. She ran past him into the bathroom, locking the door behind her. She splashed water on her red face and moaned as she sat down.

CC looked around the small bathroom. Wet towels hung over the shower rod and lay on the floor. The sink was full of shaving cream. Her mind flashed back to her life with John Reeney. She felt bad for Rachel as she scrubbed the sink and picked up the towels.

There was a knock on the door. She peeked out. Standing outside the door, Anne was dressed. "CC, coming down for breakfast?"

"Give me a few minutes," CC said, closing the door again.

Later, she sat down at the breakfast nook table, trying not to make eye contact with Jeremy, who sat directly across from her, sipping his coffee and smiling. She could feel the blush returning to her cheeks. She thought he didn't really have much to smile about, which made her smirk and made her feel a bit better.

"Jeremy, what do you do?" Anne asked, stirring three lumps of sugar into her coffee.

He put his coffee cup down again. "I work with Rachel at the museum. I'm director of marketing."

"Did you and Rachel meet at the museum?"

"We met at a Civil War Reenactment in Gettysburg."

"How cute," Anne exclaimed. "You both are reenactors?"

Rachel smiled. "Yes, I'm a Southern Belle, and Jeremy was a Union captain. He swept me off my feet." She put her arm around his neck and kissed his cheek.

"CC, what's wrong with you?" Anne asked.

"What are you talking about?"

"You keep looking at your phone."

"I was waiting for an email from work."

Anne leaned in. "You're being very rude," she whispered.

"Jeremy was working with Lindsey on the special Keckley exhibit. They were photographing the dresses for a brochure." Rachel paused. "I can't believe she is gone."

The room was quiet as if no one knew how to respond. Rachel brought over a bowl of scrambled eggs and sat down.

"Lindsey never mentioned our Keckley dress to you?" CC asked Jeremy.

He shook his head. "No."

"Why wouldn't she have told you that she was coming to our auction?" Anne asked. The words hung in the air; nobody reached for them.

Jeremy sipped his coffee, and Rachel doled out the scrambled eggs.

After the girls finished breakfast, they thanked Rachel and left, heading back to their hotel. Carrying the dress bag, Anne followed CC down the long hall to their room. Fumbling through her bag, she searched for her room key as the contents fell onto the floor, scattering silk handkerchiefs, perfume bottles, letter openers, and pill boxes. "I don't understand. I don't know where it's at," she said as she bent over to collect her belongings.

Taking her key out of her pocket, CC sighed. She flung open the door and stopped on the threshold. Anne fell into CC. "What the?" Anne said, peering over CC's shoulder. The room had been torn apart, drawers flung open, their suitcase contents scattered around the floor. "CC, the dress. They came for the dress." Anne cradled the dress bag, holding it tight as if it would be wrenched from her arms. Then she had a disturbing thought. Her purchases from earlier. Where they still here? She pushed past CC, who grabbed her and pulled her back in the hallway.

"What are you doing? It's a crime scene. You can't go back in there."

"But. . .but. . .I wanted to make sure they were still here,"

Anne stuttered.

CC took Anne by the hand and led her to the elevator. Out of the corner of her eye, she swore she saw the door leading to the stairway click shut. Her first impulse was to check the door to see who was on the other side. Then she thought of the night in the Lincoln Inn. She thought of Lindsey Kelly and her allergic reaction. She thought of Anne and the fallen armoire. All accidents or not? Anne was right. Somebody came for the dress. The elevator pinged, breaking her thoughts. They headed down to the lobby.

The manager greeted them with a smile. "Hello ladies. How can I help you?"

Anne stuttered. "Crime scene. My shopping bags."

"Excuse me," he replied, raising his eyebrows.

CC interrupted. "Our room was broken into."

Back Home, Spoon Sisters Blog

*D*EAR FRIENDS,
    It's good to be back home. So much adventure in such a short time. There was an incident at the hotel. Our room was broken into. Nothing was stolen, but Anne and I believe they were searching for the dress. Luckily, Anne kept it with her, not wanting to part with it. We are both fine. In fact, this tragedy has strengthened our resolve to discover the mystery of the dress. I fear we are not alone in this endeavor. I appreciate all the comments from you, our friends, offering assistance. Dr. Smart, particularly, if you are reading this blog, I would greatly like to speak with you.

    On to the business of the day. We are spending the day at the Bee's Knees, bringing Ingrid up to speed and preparing for business as usual."

Anne interrupted, "CC, can you finish that later? We're waiting."

CC sighed and typed.

For now, I must go. Dear friends, toodooloo.

The large oak farmhouse table was a gathering place for Anne, CC, and Ingrid. Anne sat at the far end, tapping her foot, scrolling through her iPhone. Her eBay watch list was growing by the moment. Immediately to her right, a high-back wooden chair had the dress flung over it. "Tell me, CC, how did it go? Anne was very sketchy on the details when she got home last night," Ingrid said.

CC pushed down on the French roast press, sipped her coffee. "The dress is real. It's an Elizabeth Keckley. We believe Isobel Grant worked at Keckley's school for runaway slaves."

"They're not getting the dress." Anne glanced up from her iPhone, her eyes blazing red.

"Who's not getting the dress?" Ingrid asked.

"They're not," Anne repeated.

CC got up and walked down the long table, her fingers gliding over the sawn oak top. She put her arm around Anne. "Annie, are you OK?"

"Yes, I'm fine." Anne flipped her phone around to show CC. "Next weekend, this is where we are headed. Officer's Ball in Galena by U.S Grant's house. General Grant. Isobel Grant."

"Anne, what are you talking about?"

"I'm going, and I'm wearing the dress."

"Actually, Anne, that's not a bad idea. The Civil War reenactment groups thoroughly research the time period to make sure the details are exact. They know the battles, the formations, the medicine."

"And the dresses?" Anne said.

"Can I go? That sounds like fun," Ingrid said.

"Yes, of course you can go," Anne said. "I've already contacted the society president. She is familiar with our store and our blog. She said we are welcome to attend the ball. They've offered to loan us several ball gowns, period correct. I'm sure we can find something for both of you."

While CC and Ingrid served customers at the restaurant, Anne headed out to visit an estate sale in the area. The house was a small, raised ranch, not normally worth her time, but the online pictures had shown a collection of vintage lingerie. One of their fans was interested. She saw the familiar shade of blue as she walked up the front driveway. "Buttersworth," she muttered.

Entering the home, she saw her archrival sorting through boxes of costume jewelry. "Buttersworth," she said.

"Hillstrom," was Buttersworth's reply as she dropped the aurora borealis necklace she was holding. "You're back from your vacation."

"It wasn't a vacation. It was business." Anne reached down and grabbed the necklace. It would be stunning with her new dress.

"How is business at Great-Aunt Sybil's?" Betsy asked.

"Fine," Anne replied.

"You seem to be a bit slow, but then again I don't have a lot of time to notice. The sweet shop has been overflowing." Betsy gave her a sly glance. "I bet I know what you came for."

Anne caught her glance; her eyes darted upstairs where the lingerie would be. She rushed up the stairs, Buttersworth on her heels. It brought back memories of their battle over the pants. Anne ran down the narrow second floor hallway, darting her head in bedrooms. The last bedroom had the lingerie displayed on the queen-size bed. Anne scooped it all up, not stopping to examine anything as Buttersworth burst into the room.

"Really? You need all those?" she asked.

"Buttersworth, you can afford anything you want." Anne sat down on the edge of the bed, arms full of negligees, slips and robes.

Buttersworth sat down next to her. "You know, I'm just having fun with you, Anne. I enjoy the thrill of the hunt, the high of the find just as much as you. It's not that I need anything."

"Well, but I do need these things. I have people counting on me to find orphaned artifacts. To bring them to a good home. This is my purpose in life, Betsy, what's yours?"

Buttersworth stood up, pacing about the room. "That's just it, Anne. I don't think I've found it yet. Failed marriages. Failed businesses. Things to fill the void. Distractions to fill the time. The only man I think I ever really loved is gone."

"What are you talking about?"

"Nigel."

"You barely dated."

"That's not the point. We had a real connection."

Anne began counting to ten out loud, her lips crunched guttural noises, sifting through her teeth. "Don't start, Buttersworth. You know I was, I am, in love with Nigel. Wherever he is, whatever he's doing, he's thinking about me."

"If he's thinking about you, where is he, Anne? Has he called? Has he written?"

Anne thought for a moment. When Betsy opened up herself, she became just a tiny bit more human like the Grinch. There might be a chance to rekindle their friendship, but Betsy had struck a match to the one nerve that Anne could not extinguish. She had brought up Nigel, the very tall and very British detective Nigel Towers. Anne's true love, her Wesley. Now he was gone. Perhaps like the Wesley from *The Princess Bride*, he was abducted by the Dread Pirate Roberts. She shook off the image of Nigel in a pirate's costume and stood up to face Buttersworth. "I win this time, Buttersworth." Anne left the room, this time carrying the trail of silk. She wouldn't cry in front of Buttersworth. She paid for the lingerie and left in a huff. A whole day ruined. She threw everything in the back of her Mercedes SUV. She dialed Nigel's number, but there was no answer, the same as the other hundred times she had called since he left. She opened the back door and stuck her arm underneath the driver's seat. She pulled out the Union Jack scarf, the one she had given Nigel when they first met. She enjoyed his moments of whimsy, his flower festooned ties, his bowler hats, his attempts at moustaches and beards. They had met under such dire circumstances, only to form a special friendship—that friendship blossomed into love. She smelled the scarf. She stuck her nose deep into the Irish wool. She could smell the English Leather, another gift of whimsy she had given him. She could smell his musk.

A tap on the window made her jump in her seat. Betsy motioned for her to roll down her window.

Anne pulled the scarf down quickly and lowered the window. "Cheerio," Betsy said with a smile before walking away, holding up several shopping bags.

"Buttersworth," Anne muttered.

A storm was rolling in, and the sky had turned black. Anne drove toward the farm, eager to show Ingrid her purchases. The gravel road kicked up under her tires. Lightning struck, followed by thunder. Anne counted the seconds in between the flash and the boom. Lightning struck again, but this time the thunder came quicker. She did the math. The speed of sound divided by the speed she was traveling. Flashes lit up the sky mere feet from her truck. She slammed on the brakes, sliding into the drainage ditch. Anne's heart pounded. She stepped on the gas pedal, tires spun; she pressed harder and harder. She reached for her phone and jumped when it rang. She stared at the icon, not believing it. It rang again. Nigel's face appeared on her FaceTime. The image of the Union Jack gave way to a very gawky chin. "Nigel, is that you?"

"Annie, can you see me?"

"Lift the phone higher, Nigel."

"How's that?" A face appeared. He looked tired. He looked older.

"Nigel, I've been trying to get in touch with you since you left."

"I was not allowed to have any conversations, Annie, I'm so sorry. I shouldn't be speaking with you now."

"Nigel, what are you talking about? Where are you?"

"Annie, I'm not at liberty to say. It was a family emergency, that's all they will allow me to say."

"Who is 'they'? Nigel?" Anne asked as his face flickered. Then the screen went black. A message saying "audio only" appeared. "Nigel, just tell me, where you are? I'll come to you. I can help."

"In due time, Annie." His voice crackled, and then the connection was lost.

Anne hit redial only to get a fast busy signal. She tried again and again and again until she finally threw the phone down. Anne's head throbbed. A heavy rain pounded on the windshield. She could barely see through the deluge. Her throat itched. Her eyes began to water. She coughed. Anne cleared her throat; her eyes burned. She reached under the seat, grabbed Nigel's scarf, and took another whiff. English Leather, Nigel musk, and a licorice smell. Goldenrod, the one plant she was allergic to. She sneezed three times and stuffed the scarf back under the seat. She remembered the day Nigel had worn it. It had been their last picnic, early fall. They sat on the lawn at the Peabody Mansion, overlooking the stage, watching a performance of The *Taming of the Shrew*. With the scarf wrapped around his neck, Nigel sat with his long bony legs outstretched, resting on his bony elbows. She had not noticed the goldenrod behind the bushes where they sat until she began uncontrollably sneezing. The scarf. She sneezed loudly. The scarf. Lindsey wasn't wearing a scarf!

A tap on the window startled Anne. Looking up, she saw Nigel peering in at her. His long, bony face pressed against the glass.

She closed her eyes and shook her head. When she opened her eyes, the state trooper stared back at her. "Are you ok, ma'am?" he asked.

"Not so much," Anne said.

On to Galena, Spoon Sisters Blog

*D*EAR FRIENDS,
    Today, we're heading to Galena, Illinois. Established in 1826, Galena was named after galena, which is the mineral form of lead sulfide. In the 19th century, Galena became the busiest port on the Mississippi between St. Paul and St. Louis. Interesting fact: Native Americans mined the ore for use in burial rituals.

In 1832, Daniel Smith Harris and his brother Robert Scrib began construction on the Jo-Daviess steamboat, the first steamboat built on the Fever River near Galena. Then the Blackhawk War broke out. Indians defeated the militia at the battle of Stillmen's Run. The stockade was built in Galena as settlers flocked to the town.

To Anne's delight, it is known as the antique capitol of the Midwest, blocks and blocks of antique stores along the river, with 19th century beds-and-breakfasts peeking from the hilltops above. She hopes to visit every shop. Anne is already scouring the websites of the local stores looking for items on our request list.

There is a very active Civil War re-enactment group in Galena. Adding to Anne's excitement, we have been invited to attend a Civil War-era ball, costumes required. Anne will be wearing her Keckley dress. I will be sure to take many pictures and share them with you. I'm sure this will be a very rewarding trip.

Until next time, dear friends, toodooloo.

CC glanced up from her laptop. Anne was peeking over her shoulder in the small kitchenette at Great-Aunt Sybil's Attic. Ingrid rushed down the stairs from Anne's apartment, carrying Anne's suitcase. "Are you done? We have to get going. We're going to be late," Anne said.

They packed the bus and headed out on the highway. Ingrid leaned forward from the back seat, and Anne read out loud. "Galena has some of the most impressive 19th century buildings, like the 1826 Dowling house."

"That's right," CC interrupted. "John Dowling arrived in Galena in 1826. He built his limestone house in a single-pen style."

"What's that?" Ingrid asked.

"A single pen is one unit: a rectangle of four walls of a log cabin," CC said. "The first floor was a trading post while the Dowlings lived upstairs. By 1838, he was a town trustee," CC continued, "The whole town is full of history. We'll have to stop at Grant's house. President Grant's home was designed by William Dennison in 1860. The home was given to Grant by residents of Galena as a thank you for his war service, but Ingrid, most important thing of all, Galena is the antique center of the Midwest."

Anne interrupted, "It's mecca, Ingrid, mecca. Almost every store that lines both sides of the street is an antique shop. Above the antique shops on the hills are beds and breakfasts, turn-of-the century or older. I could live there, Ingrid, I could live there."

"We're not going to have a lot of time," CC said. "We have to get our dresses and get ready for the ball tonight."

"Luckily for us, Millie, one of the ladies from the Civil War Society and the one who has dresses for you to try on, also owns an antique store down Main Street. It's called Millie's Bygones. Adorable, don't you think?"

Ingrid smiled.

"We can stop, try on dresses, look around, and walk up and down the street until it's time for the ball. And I've read about a delightful little bistro called Fritz & Frites. It's a little German, a little French, sounds delightful," Anne said. She thought for a moment. "CC, have you thought about what I said last night?" she whispered. "Lindsey wasn't wearing a scarf when we found her." Anne checked the rearview mirror to see Ingrid bopping her head with her earbuds in.

"She had a fatal allergic reaction. Her throat was swollen. If she was wearing a scarf, don't you think the first thing she would do would be to take it off?"

"That's just the thing. I don't remember seeing it anywhere around the hotel room."

"Maybe it was hanging in the closet."

"No, I checked the closet. Every outfit had a matching scarf." Anne had thought and thought. She could remember every item in Lindsey's closet or strewn on the dresser. She did not recall a stray scarf.

"Lindsey had an allergic reaction to latex. She must have come in contact with it somehow."

"How do you know that?"

"I read the coroner's report."

"When was this? How did you get all this information?"

"I'm a journalist."

"How come you waited until now to tell me?" Anne asked.

"There's something else I didn't tell you. The night you were in the hospital, somebody tried to break into my hotel room. At least I think that's what happened."

"CC."

"I know you feel responsible for Lindsey because she came to see your dress. I didn't want to put this all on you. We can tell the police about the scarf, but most likely they won't comment on an ongoing investigation," CC said.

"When has this all been going on? Where have I been? Why aren't you including me in on your investigation?"

"It's not an investigation. I made a couple of calls, that's it. I've been worried about you since the armoire fell on you. You have a concussion."

"What are you saying?" Anne remembered the lovely Majorelle armoire. She wondered if it was still at the store, and if it was, would they take layaway. And if they did take layaway, where she could put it? It was a little large for her tiny apartment.

"I'm saying that someone is willing to kill for that dress, Anne."

"Whatever's going to happen, we're going to go through it together. No more secrets, ok?"

"What are you two talking about?" Ingrid popped her head in between the seats.

"Turn here," Anne yelled. "Turn here."

CC hung a hard left and slowed down, giving them their first glimpse of Galena.

Anne gasped. Blocks and blocks of antique stores, all waiting her arrival. She couldn't wait to begin her assault, planning her attack. She pointed to the address of Millie's Bygones.

The line of customers stretched around the block as CC maneuvered the VW into a narrow space in front of the building. "She must be having a huge sale," Anne said as she jumped out of the car and dashed toward the end of the line.

"She's here." Anne heard the whispers as she waited in line.

"Are you Anne Hillstrom?" Voices buzzed around her. "The Anne Hillstrom? Of course, you are. I recognize you from your pictures on the blog. I can't believe you're here."

CC and Ingrid came to stand next to Anne in the line. "You don't have to wait in line," the woman said again to Anne. "We're all here for you."

"Really, I'm so flattered," Anne said, stepping onto the street, facing the crowd and giving a little curtsy. The fans, their fans, applauded.

A young frazzled woman came out of the shop and walked up to Anne. "Good afternoon, Miss Hillstrom, I'm Millie." She took her by the arm and led her into the shop. CC and Ingrid followed.

"What's this all about?" Anne asked.

"I posted on our web page and Facebook that the Spoon Sisters were coming to my store in Galena. They all showed up." Millie held out a tray of freshly baked lemon cookies.

Anne bit into one and sighed, savoring the sweet tang of citrus. It was delicious. She reached for another. "This is a wonderful store you have. I noticed you have some primitives."

"Yes, I collect them myself."

"I love these 18th century needlework pieces." Anne admired the table display of samplers.

"Oh, you noticed. I'm a big fan of antique needlepoint." Millie waved to the crowd outside. "I hope you don't mind, but a lot of people brought antiques with them hoping you would appraise them. I know this is last minute. They wanted to get your opinion on some of their treasures. I could set up a table for you."

"We have to. . ." Anne looked at CC who nodded her approval.

"Of course, that would be wonderful."

Ingrid helped Millie bring a table into the center of the store and set two chairs behind it. Anne browsed through the rows of clothes, fingering the soft silk, rustled taffeta, and homespun cotton of a bygone age. She held a linen day dress trimmed with lace up to her, spreading its wide skirt out. A waltz hummed in her head. She pictured Nigel in his cavalry uniform, bowing.

"Anne, Anne," CC interrupted her train of fantasy. "They're coming in. Sit down. We can try on dresses later."

The stream flowed in one by one, each one carrying a precious treasure. Anne was in her element, carefully handling these precious heirlooms. One fan carried a box full of car models sealed in their original boxes. CC could barely contain her excitement. "I haven't seen these since I was a little girl," she said.

"Yes, they've been in our basement. My father and brother used to put them together. These are what they didn't have time for," the woman said.

"Well, the prices vary, ranging from twelve dollars to forty dollars, depending on which model it is. For example, this 1965 Mustang is probably the most valuable, and these are still popular today," CC said.

"I couldn't sell them. My brother died in Desert Storm, and this is all I have of his," the woman said.

"It's a wonderful collection," CC said.

"Thank you, " the woman said, taking the box and moving out of line.

CC smiled at the next woman who carried a necklace of bear claws.

Anne shuddered.

"Hi, my name is Mary. I'm a big fan," she said, pulling out a LaCrosse stick.

CC examined both items. "Hi, Mary. The Sauk Indians played stickball which became Lacrosse. The young men in the clans were divided into two major ceremonial groups called moieties. As many as 100 to 1000 men participated in the games." CC turned back to the woman who had brought the items. "How did you get these?"

"My great-great-great-grandfather fought against Chief Blackhawk during the war. He was a major in the militia and stationed at Fort Apple River," she said.

"These are quite valuable," CC said.

"I also have some things that belonged to my great-great-great-grandmother." She pulled several beaded purses out of her bag.

Anne reached for the elaborate flowered one with its mauve and yellow design. Its fringe dangled delicately from the square bottom. "These are beautiful," she said. "The beads are glass, and it's in amazing condition." She opened the clasp. "The interior is in excellent condition, too. Some yellowing but it's not torn."

"Thank you. Do you know what the purses are worth?"

"I'd say this one a couple hundred dollars." Anne pointed to the smaller day bag and then to the more elaborate one. "This one is probably worth at least a thousand dollars. I'd love to add it to my personal collection."

Mary hesitated. "I hate to part with it. It's been in our family so very long." She stopped and thought. "But my husband's been out of work, and we could use the money."

Anne wrote the woman a check, placing the purse in a growing pile on the side of the table.

"Will I see you tonight at the ball?" Mary turned and asked Anne.

"Oh, are you part of the Society?"

"Yes, I play Mary Todd Lincoln. My great-great-great-grandmother met Mary Todd when she lived in Batavia."

"Oh, then she must have known Elizabeth Keckley."

"No, Miss Keckley stopped working for Mary Todd when she left the White House."

"They never had any correspondence after that?"

"Not that I know of, and I've done quite a bit of research since I play her every year. They were estranged by the time Miss Keckley published her memoirs."

"I know."

"I've been following your search to authenticate the dress on your blog. You know that Mary Todd sold off many of her dresses after the president was assassinated. For a long time, she fought to receive a pension from the government, blaming them for everything that happened to her husband. She was obsessed about becoming indigent. She walked around Chicago with thousands of dollars sewn into her dresses."

"Yes, I know. I already checked my dress. No such luck."

"You should really go to Bellevue house to research Mary Todd's later days. I've become fast friends with the manager."

"We'll have to do that. Thank you so much," Anne said.

The line of fans thinned out. CC and Ingrid searched the racks for dresses to wear to the ball. Ingrid tried on dress after dress, each one fitting her slim figure perfectly. She finally settled on a sage green silk with a white ruffled skirt. CC fixated on a somber black gown.

Haunted House, Spoon Sisters Blog

D*EAR FRIENDS,*
Thank you so much for coming out today to welcome us to Galena. We were overwhelmed by your enthusiasm and generosity. So many wonderful antiques and heirlooms. And, Millie, what a wonderful hostess. She made us feel right at home. A kindred spirit of rust and dust. For those of you unable to attend, I've uploaded many photos from Millie's store and our fans.

Anne was able to check off many items on our request list. We will be contacting those lucky recipients by PM. Anne also added several items to her personal collection. She asked me to share this photo of the beaded handbag she had to have and will be carrying tonight. Ingrid found the perfect dress for the ball tonight. She is such a beautiful young woman. I'm so very proud of her. I've included a photo of me in my ball gown selection. I hope it's flattering.

A little bit about where we are staying tonight. We have chosen the DeSoto House, which is advertised as the most haunted house in the Midwest. Maybe we'll see spirits tonight or at least drink some. For now I must get ready. Until next time, toodooloo."

Spanning an entire block, the DeSoto House's exterior was ablaze with light. Strains of music filtered out onto the sidewalk. Anne danced as they made their way to the front entrance of the hotel. "President Lincoln gave a speech here in 1856 to support John Fremont's presidential run," CC said. "And then Ulysses Grant used the house as his campaign headquarters."

"That is all true," Millie said, leading the way through the hotel lobby. "It has been restored magnificently, wouldn't you say? We use it for our annual Society fundraising ball, but I must warn you it is haunted."

"I've read about that," CC said.

"It's true," Millie said. "I've personally smelled cigars and heard whispered secrets in the hallway. When it was restored, the guest rooms were made larger so walls were moved and built over the old hallways. Current guests claim they see people coming in and out of those walls." Millie smiled as she led them into the ballroom.

Anne stood in the entrance to the ballroom, a young Abraham Lincoln towered over all the attendees, greeting each with a smile and a hearty handshake. Mary greeted them. "Ladies, let me introduce you to my husband, President Abraham Lincoln."

Abraham removed his stovetop hat, placed his arm across his waist, and bowed. "Welcome, fine ladies, to Galena. You are most welcome," he said.

As CC discussed steamships, Anne admired the crystal chandeliers, the marble floor, the arched windows. She caught a glance of herself reflected in the hall gilded mirror. The navy blue dress accented the blue in her eyes, the jet beads sparkled in the light. She stared at the gawky Lincoln impersonator. Another two inches taller and he would match Nigel's stature. Although he had neither the charm nor the elegance of a Nigel Towers. She could feel his bony arms around her as she danced in the entryway, imagining General Nigel Towers of the Illinois Cavalry in his dashing blues.

"Excuse me, ma'am, you seem to have started without a partner. May I step in?"

Anne gasped as she turned to see a handsome General Grant, holding out his hand to her. She curtseyed, raising her hand to be kissed. The general obliged and walked her into the ballroom.

CC stood with the wallflowers as they fanned themselves and gossiped about the day's events. Ingrid was surrounded by young suitors much like Scarlett O'Hara, keeping them at bay while encouraging their attention with her batting eyelashes and reserved smile.

Anne twirled around with Ulysses. She found herself lost in time. She had never been a child of the twenty-first century. Her heart was in the past, touching history through antiques, transporting her in a Vernian time machine set for the Gilded Age, Belle Epoque or Art Deco era or even deeper back into history. As the waltz ended, Anne stopped and clapped. She curtseyed to the general and headed for some punch.

"Your dress is beautiful. It looks so authentic."

"Thank you," Anne said as she ladled punch, filling her crystal cup. She turned to see a woman her age, her ebony skin radiated against the yellow of her ball gown. Her auburn hair piled high. Anne smiled. "It is authentic. It's an Elizabeth Keckley."

The woman gasped. "You're not serious, are you? How did you ever?"

"I'm an antique hunter. I'm Anne Hillstrom by the way," she said, giving her hand.

"Of course, you are. I saw you at Millie's place today. We didn't have a chance to speak. I'm Gloria Brown. I've been with the group for ten years. I love to dress up."

"Does everyone play a real-life character? I danced with General Grant, met Mr. Lincoln."

"Some of us who have been here since the beginning play notable figures from the era. Others just period correct dress and manner."

"What about you?"

"I do play a character. Her name is Izzy Washington. She was a schoolteacher who smuggled slaves up north through the Underground Railroad."

"Schoolteacher? Where did she teach?"

"Izzy began teaching on a plantation in Maryland. The owner of the plantation would send her to other plantations for a fee to teach some of their house slaves."

"Teach them what?"

"Reading was not allowed. Some were taught French and mathematics. Things that would help around the house and often to teach the owners' children."

"Very interesting," Anne said. "Have you ever heard of Isobel Grant? I believe she was a teacher also. She helped teach runaway slaves in Washington."

" The name's not familiar."

"I thought maybe because she taught runaway slaves in Washington."

"Was she a slave?"

Anne thought for a moment. "I never even considered that. I assumed she was a woman of Washington society. This was her dress."

"My dress is modeled after one I saw of a picture of Izzy. After years of teaching, she saved enough money to buy her freedom. She continued teaching slaves in the free North."

"In Washington?"

"I believe she was in Washington at one point."

"That's fascinating. I'd love to learn more."

"My husband's waving to me for a dance. Are you in town very long?"

"Just the night. We're staying in this hotel."

"Oh, you are? What room are you in?"

"333."

Gloria's smile flew away.

"What's wrong?" Anne asked.

"Do you know the history of the hotel?"

"Yes, I know it's supposed to be haunted, but I don't believe in that nonsense." Anne waved off the concerns, trying to put on a brave face.

"That's good because Room 333 is the most haunted room in the whole hotel, in fact in the whole Midwest. People claim to have been woken up in the middle of the night by someone sitting on their bed. The shadow figure stood up and walked through the walls."

Anne's hand shook, spilling her punch. "Oh my goodness." She put the crystal cup down.

"Nice speaking with you, Anne. " Gloria glided past Anne as she was still absorbing the sentence that hung in the air—the most haunted room in the Midwest.

The night flew by in a whirlwind of quadrilles and waltzes. Anne do-si-doed in accompaniment to the caller's commands. Her head swirled from the punch, the music, and the twirling on the dance floor. She felt dizzy and took a seat by the wall. As the caller announced the final dance, the Virginia Reel, a handsome Union soldier bowed and reached out his hand, not saying a word. Anne looked up, seeing double. She rubbed her eyes. The handsome man stood silent, waiting for her acceptance. Anne smiled and took his hand which was ice cold. She thought how nervous he must be asking her to dance which made her feel good about herself, so she agreed. She was swept into the circle of dancers, his strong arms guiding her. He stared deep into her eyes. It made Anne feel uncomfortable. She felt as if she were cheating on Nigel. Anne still managed a flirting smile. After all, Nigel had left her, not at the altar but at the doorway of what could have been a happy ending. The young soldier did not smile back. There seemed to be a sadness, a distance in his stare. At the final strain of the violin, he bowed to Anne. She curtseyed back. As she lifted her eyes, she watched him disappear into the wall. She stared after him, stumbling to the wall, pounding on it, searching for a secret passage.

"CC, did you see that?" Anne grabbed her friend's arm and pointed to the wall.

"What?"

"My partner, he, went through there," she stuttered.

"Through where? There's no door."

"That's what I'm saying. He walked through the wall."

CC moved up close, peering into Anne's eyes. "How much punch did you have?"

"Maybe six, maybe seven cups." She had lost count of how many of the tiny cups she had. She had been hot from dancing, and the punch had gone down easy. Anne began to swoon – CC grabbed her by the arm.

"Do you want to sit down? Can I get you some water?"

"No, get me a punch." She reached out her arm, grasping for the small crystal cup.

"No, I think you've had enough. Why don't we head up to our room?" CC led her friend up the stairs to their third floor room. "Here we are, 333."

"No, CC, no." Anne stopped in the threshold. "This is the most haunted room in the Midwest. I don't want to sleep in there."

"Don't be silly. That is just a myth, an urban legend."

Anne hiccupped. "The wall. The soldier walked through the wall," she said, slurring her woods.

CC helped her through the door, hanging onto Anne as she removed her own shoes. The thick green carpet squished between her toes. She led Anne over to the paisley-patterned wing back chair which stood guard by the palladium window. The moonlight snuck in through the sheers. CC knelt down and pulled off Anne's heels. "Anne, I've been thinking about Batavia and Bellevue Place."

"Yes?" Anne asked.

"I think we should take a trip."

"Trip? That sounds great," Anne said, slurring her words and letting out a big yawn.

CC helped Anne out of her dress and tucked her into her double bed. She carefully laid both dresses over the wing back chairs and sat at the small writing desk. She flipped open her MacBook and began typing.

The Ball,
Spoon Sisters Blog

*D*EAR FRIENDS,
    What an adventure today. Anne and I enjoyed our visit to Galena, the antique capital of Illinois. Unfortunately, we had limited time so we were not able to find as many items on our list as we would have liked to. Anne promises to come back though. The Civil War Reenactment Society Ball was splendid. I'm including pictures of Anne and me in our ball gowns. Also one of Ingrid dancing.

CC smiled as she looked at Anne's picture. She hit zoom and then zoomed in again. Behind Anne's right shoulder, a bright orb floated. "Just a trick of the light," she said aloud.

CC returned to her typing.

Tomorrow we head to Batavia, Illinois, and the Bellevue Place to research Mary Todd's stay at the sanitarium. I know I've only given you bits and pieces of the mystery, but until now I thought it little more than a mystery. Until next time, toodooloo.

She stopped typing, glanced at Anne who was snoring softly and said, "I realize now that it's a murder mystery."

She closed her laptop with a click, erasing the image of the floating orb from her mind and replacing it with the image of her boyfriend, Nick. His raven black hair, his five o'clock shadow, his midnight eyes, the smell of smoke and musk. He had never finished his question. She closed her eyes and was startled by the phone vibrating. She grabbed it off the nightstand. "Hello," she asked, checking the time. It was 1 a.m.

"CC, it's Rachel."

"What's wrong?" CC sat up and switched on the light next to the bed. Anne stirred slightly, moaning in her sleep.

"I couldn't wait to call you," Rachel's voice signaled her urgency. "The seal on the invoice with Isobel Grant."

"Yes."

"The seal is President Lincoln's secretary, John Hay's."

"That means President Lincoln must have approved the invoice," CC said.

"It was illegal at that time to teach slaves to read, so that means a sitting president was breaking the law. This was months before he signed the Emancipation Proclamation."

"Well, thank you, that's something to think about, but this could have waited until morning."

"I looked through the boxes of letters after you left and found more information on Isobel Grant. She was a slave owned by a Virginia plantation owner, Thomas Pickett."

"What was she doing in Washington and helping with the school for runaway slaves? Was she a runaway herself?" CC found herself waking up.

"No, that's the most interesting fact. I found several letters of travel allowing her to cross between Confederate and Union borders. The same seal was on those letters—John Hay's. Pickett was murdered towards the end of the Civil War. It was never determined who killed him. His son, Zachary, sold the plantation and moved to Illinois."

"Does it say where he moved to?"

"Batavia. He was also found murdered in 1901. I read the police report, an apparent home invasion."

"What happened to Isobel?"

"I can't find any other record of her. I was worried about you and Anne. I had to call right away. CC, that dress has left a trail of dead bodies for more than a hundred and fifty years. Be careful."

"Thank you, Rachel." CC put her phone down, turned off the light and tried to go back to sleep. She tossed and turned, watching the clock. Loud voices outside her room startled her. She coughed from the cigar smoke. Shaking her head in disbelief, she covered her face with the pillow. A vision came to her of a decomposing Isobel Grant wearing the dress in a shallow grave. CC whispered the words of Edgar Allan Poe, "Sleep, those little slices of death—how I loathe them." Her eyes flew open. A grave robber slipped in and stole CC's slice of death. No sleep for her, this night would come. She lay awake until the sun came peeking through the sheers.

Anne sat upright in her bed, gasping for air.

"What's wrong, Anne?"

"Nightmare. I had a nightmare."

"How's your head, Anne?" CC asked, as she started the coffeepot.

"It's much better. I might have overdone it with the punch last night."

CC handed Anne a black coffee, which she sipped tentatively. After they drank their coffee, they both rushed to pack their things, neither wanting to stay in Room 333, a second longer than necessary.

Anne stretched out on the green and white vinyl seats of the VW's front while Ingrid slept in the backbench seat. She missed her luxurious deep leather seats of her Mercedes, but CC insisted on driving the official Spoon Sisters road trip van. It always made Anne think of the Mystery Van of Scooby Doo but in this world the monsters were real.

"So, Rachel believes that Isobel Grant was a slave who held traveling papers and taught at a school for runaway slaves in Washington?"

CC nodded, keeping her eyes straight on the road.

"And her master, Thomas Pickett, was found murdered near the end of the war? And his son was also found murdered in Batavia where we are headed?"

"Yes."

"Do you think Sharon Prima was related to Thomas Pickett?" Anne asked.

"How else would she have wound up with the dress?"

"Why would Pickett travel to Batavia all the way from Virginia?"

"Mary Todd Lincoln was committed by Robert Todd to the sanitarium for disturbed women in Batavia, Bellevue Place. There's a connection between Mary Todd and Thomas Pickett. A thread that binds their fate, that thread was used to sew your dress."

Anne reached around to the back seat, touching the dress bag. She felt the bag from the Kelly's Originals store. She took the cloche hat out and placed it on her head. "What do you think, CC?"

CC glanced sideways. "It's cute. I like it."

Anne took the driving hat off to admire it. She plucked a single black hair off, staring at it.

"What's wrong?" CC asked.

"Somebody must have tried it on before me. There's a black hair. Maybe I should take it to the cleaners before I put it back on." Anne examined the hair closer. "I don't think this is human."

"What do you mean?"

"It looks like a cat hair." Anne should know. She was normally covered in white cat hair, courtesy of Sassy and Sybil.

"Reina and Luna were in the van. It's possible they shed somewhere."

"They were in crates. Even if a hair fell out of the crate, this hat has been in the bag until just now."

"Connie doesn't have cats. It's possible the hair was from another customer that tried it on or maybe the person she bought it from."

Anne took the tiny hair, grabbed a tissue from her purse and wrapped it up carefully before placing it in her bag.

Batavia Bound,
Spoon Sisters Blog

*D*EAR FRIENDS,
We are back at Great-Aunt Sybil's. Ingrid plans to open the store today while Anne and I head to Batavia to visit the Bel-levue Place, once home to Mary Todd Lincoln. I thank so many of you for sending information about the former First Lady. Judith from Chicago shared this about Mrs. Lincoln's stay in Chicago. In front of a small building in Chicago at 1232 W. Washington St. hangs an old historical marker from 1937. It reads, "Mrs. Lincoln's home." I've uploaded the picture she sent so you can see it. It reads, "On this site stood the home of Mrs. Abraham Lincoln, bought in 1866 and occupied for about a year with her son, Tad. She did not stay in the row house long because she was continuously trying to raise money to pay off her $20,000 in shopping debts, which she had concealed from her husband. She sold off some of her furniture to the Hyde Park Hotel for $2,094.50. The furniture burned with the hotel in the late 1870s. Thank you, Judith. From all I've read, Mary Todd became mentally unstable with her constant dread of living in poverty. She didn't trust banks. She would sew money into her dresses, hide it about the house, which leads me to believe Anne's dress is somehow related to Mrs. Lincoln's obsession.

She paused to read a comment, popping up from Dr. Smart. CC read, "On October 11, 2012, young Miriam went to a party with her new boyfriend. After a couple drinks, she went to her boyfriend's place about 3 a.m. While Miriam went to the bedroom, her boyfriend stopped in the kitchen to eat a piece of toast with peanut butter. He then brushed his teeth and joined his new girlfriend. After they kissed, Miriam felt unwell and used her

Ventolin inhaler. When that didn't help, she asked her boyfriend if he had peanut butter—he was not aware of her allergy. When he told her about the toast, she said to call 9-1-1. While he was on the phone with the dispatcher, her symptoms progressed. She did not have her EpiPen. The dispatcher had the young man start CPR. The ambulance arrived in eight minutes. She was immediately administered an EpiPen. Her throat was so inflamed they couldn't insert a breathing tube. She suffered cardiopulmonary failure in the ambulance and died. Even though this was an accidental death from an allergic reaction, imagine if this was murder."

CC's heart pounded. It wasn't the first time a killer used anaphylaxis shock as a weapon. What disturbed her even more was this Dr. Smart and why he was sending her these comments. Who was he? And what were his intentions? Why was he confiding in her? What did he know?

She shook off the uncomfortable feeling and returned to typing.

Today, we hope to find some clues to back that theory. We will fill you in as soon as we are able. Until then, dear friends, toodooloo.

A short while later, Anne and CC stared at a large Greek revival building. Its sign proclaimed, "Bellevue Place Apartments." "You know, Anne, this building was built in 1854 as a private boarding high school," CC said. "It cost $15,000 to build. In 1867, Dr. Richard Patterson bought it and transformed it into a mental hospital for women."

Anne shuddered. She could almost hear the screams of the women coming from the walls.

"Sanitariums were in demand, and there was a belief that a quiet environment away from the city could cure mental illness," CC continued. "Because there were so many women distraught from losing loved ones in the Civil War. Losing her husband and three children made some people believe that Mary Todd's mental instability was due to emotional distress, but she was only here for a short time." CC pointed up. "Mary Todd's room was on the second floor."

Anne stared up at the second floor, wondering which window was the one Mary Todd looked out of. She pictured the former First Lady in her black widow's dress, overcome with grief caused by the loss of the president and her sons. Here she was committed by her remaining son. She must have felt so betrayed, so alone.

"We should go to the Batavia Depot Museum," CC interrupted Anne's thoughts. "They have some of Mary Todd's hospital records on display."

Anne felt her iPhone vibrate. She pulled it out of her bag. The bright Union Jack flashed. She sat down on the bench in front of the building. CC appeared puzzled. Anne held up her finger. "It's Nigel," she whispered. "Hello," she spoke into the phone.

A crackled voice answered her back. "Annie, is that you?"

"Nigel, yes, yes," she said, her voice becoming louder with her enthusiasm.

"Annie, I can barely hear you. The reception here is horrible."

"Where are you?" Anne asked.

"I'm not allowed to say."

"What do you mean you're not allowed to say? You've had me very worried since our last conversation. Are you in some sort of trouble?"

"No, not trouble, Anne, but still a bit of a pickle. I'm constantly being watched. I snuck away just to call you, but I'm afraid I must get back."

"Nigel, you're not making any sense."

"Annie, I miss you terribly."

"Well, Nigel, if you miss me so terribly, why did you go? Why haven't you answered any of my calls? Why is everything such a great mystery?"

"Annie, I have to go. They may be listening. I wanted to hear your voice. I wanted to let you know I'm thinking of you." The phone went dead and so did Anne's hopes. Whatever game Nigel was playing, Anne was opting out. She couldn't allow herself to open up to him again. It hurt too much.

"Are you ok?" CC asked, walking over and sitting down next to her.

"Nigel won't say where he is or what he's doing or why he left," Anne said with a sniffle. "Let's go to the Depot. I need a distraction."

"Let's walk there," CC said.

Anne trudged along behind CC. "Wait," Anne said, stopping in front of a gourmet popcorn shop called Colonel Kernel's. She stood in front of the plate glass window, watching the corn turning in the giant kettle. The smell was intoxicating, sugar and salt. Popcorn couldn't mend a broken heart, but it sure helped. Anne stepped into the store. "That smells fantastic."

The young girl making the popcorn turned and smiled. "Thank you."

Anne looked around the nineteenth century store, eying the original photographs hanging on the wall above tiny café tables. She took a closer look. "CC, take a look." One photograph showed a group of well-dressed women, obviously of some means, standing in front of what she recognized as the store she was now in. At that time, it was a dress shop. One of them was Mary Todd Lincoln.

"That's a great photograph, isn't it?" the young woman said from behind the counter. "There's a lot of photographs of Mary Todd around the village. Rumor has it the former owner of the dress shop sold some of Mary Todd's dresses. Occasionally she bought dresses from her. She frequented the store quite often searching for a particular dress, a navy blue silk day dress with jet beads."

Anne gasped, and clutched CC's arms. "How do you know that?" CC asked.

"I've got the original owner's journals from the store. I found them in the attic when we were rehabbing the place. During the months Mary Todd was in Batavia, there were notes about how she came in everyday asking about this dress."

Anne slowly reached out her hand for the bag of kettle corn and filled her mouth, wide-eyed as though watching a suspense movie.

"Could we see the journal?" CC asked. "My name's CC Muller. I'm a reporter. This is my assistant, Anne Hillstrom."

"I'm Linda, nice to meet you." She came around the counter and shook both their hands. "Living in Batavia, we've all grown up hearing stories of Mary Todd and her time here. Give me a moment, and I'll get the book." Linda stepped out of the room.

Anne sank onto one of the café chairs, munching on her popcorn.

Linda returned shortly holding a tattered leatherbound journal. She carefully placed it on the café table and sat next to Anne. CC peered over their shoulders. "It's in pretty bad shape, but you can clearly make out the name Mary Todd Lincoln."

As Linda turned the pages carefully, she pointed to each entry and then read out loud, "Mrs. Lincoln is insistent about the dress, blue silk, jet beadings about the shoulder and bodice. I've contacted several of my colleagues in Chicago, New York, and Washington." She flipped to another entry and then read, "Mrs. Lincoln continues to ramble about the dress, a dress made by her former dressmaker, Elizabeth Keckley. It must be of great value or at least hold some sentimental meaning to the distraught Mrs. Lincoln."

"Did he ever find the dress?" Anne asked.

"There's no mention of it, but he does write that Mrs. Lincoln was generally considered unstable by the townspeople. Her obsession about the dress fed into the rumors of her mental instability. A lot of the merchants reported similar interactions with the former first lady."

Anne munched on popcorn. This was better than any history book she had ever read or even watching the History Channel. Almost better than Antiques Roadshow.

"We appreciate your letting us see this," CC said. "We came to Batavia to learn more about Mary Todd's stay."

"Are you heading to the museum?" Linda asked.

"Yes, that's our next stop." CC said. They thanked Linda and stepped out onto the sidewalk. It was a few blocks to the depot museum. They strolled along the Fox River Bike Path, bikers whizzing by them. "So, what is going on with you and Nigel?"

"I don't know." Anne shrugged. "He took off without a word, and when he has reached out to me, it's been very odd. He's hiding where he is and what he's doing."

They walked into the depot museum. "You know, this used to be Batavia's Chicago, Burlington and Quincy station." They strolled through the main exhibit room which featured the history of the three rail lines that had once serviced Batavia. Then they stepped into the room showcasing famous Batavians. Next to a picture of Mary Todd Lincoln was the bed and dresser that had occupied her room at Bellevue Place.

A group of children wearing yellow shirts walked in single file and lined up around the roped-off Mary Todd exhibit. "Ok, children, spread out so everyone can see," an elderly woman wearing a Batavia Historical Society badge smiled at Anne and CC, who moved over to make room for the kids. "Mrs. Lincoln only stayed in Batavia for a short while, but she left quite an impression. These are some of the items that were in the room where she stayed. During her stay here, she hosted garden parties for the local society women. My great-grandmother actually had tea with her several times."

A little boy about ten years old raised his hand.

"Yes, Michael?"

"Mrs. Eldridge, I read Mrs. Lincoln was crazy."

"It's not a term we like to use. She was upset by the death of her husband and her sons. Batavia became her resting place, a place of sanctuary."

After a little more discussion, the children walked over to the 1907 caboose on display.

"Excuse me, Mrs. Eldridge?" Anne asked.

"Yes, dear."

"I'm Anne HIllstrom. This is my friend CC Muller. Do you have a minute? Can we ask you some questions about Mary Todd?"

"Of course, dear."

"We're here doing research. We own an antique shop in Glen Ellyn, and we have an Elizabeth Keckley dress which we are trying to discover the provenance on."

"Of course, Mary had many Keckley dresses."

"You said that your great-grandmother knew Mrs. Lincoln?" CC asked.

"That's correct. She was somewhat of a socialite herself. My great-grandfather was the administrator of the Bellevue Place when it was a sanitarium."

"That's fascinating."

"I have many letters between my great-grandmother and Mrs. Lincoln. My great-grandfather kept journals detailing her stay, along with the patient files from the doctors who treated her. Of course, back then there was no doctor/patient confidentiality."

"You have the doctor's notes from her stay?"

"My great-grandfather kept all the records from the sanitarium."

"Would it be possible for us to see those?" Anne asked.

Mrs. Eldridge smiled. "Do you like chicken pot pie? It's chicken pot pie night."

"It's my favorite," Anne said, her mouth watering at the thought of creamy chicken embraced by fresh dough.

"Why don't we make it supper, then, shall we? The museum closes at five. Let me give you my address. I would enjoy the company. I'd love to hear more about your antique store. I have quite a collection myself, many family heirlooms," Mrs. Eldridge said.

All Anne heard was chicken pot pie and antiques, and she was sold.

Baubles in Batavia, Spoon Sisters Blog

*D*EAR FRIENDS,
While we were out today, Anne discovered this quaint little antique shop charmingly named Baubles in Batavia. The store is a virtual treasure trove of costume and fine estate jewelry. Anne spent hours there, sifting through pearl necklaces, chunky gemstone pendants, and dangly earrings. In fact, Anne was so enthralled that she is still there while I write this. She found a pair of garnet earrings in a brass setting that she purchased for Lora who has been searching for a pair to wear with her grandmother's garnet pendant. For Audrey, she found a lovely pearl choker ringed with crystal to give to her daughter, Stephanie. I left her while she was deciding between an amethyst Art Nouveau brooch or a sapphire and diamond filigree ring. I assured her she needed neither, and Anne promised me that she is solely window shopping.

Once I can drag Anne away, we are headed toward dinner with a local historian whose great-grandmother knew Mrs. Lincoln. I'm so excited to learn more about Mrs. Lincoln's stay here.

Until next time, dear friends, toodooloo.

CC closed her laptop and sat back on the small metal bench outside Baubles in Batavia. Her phone rang. She recognized the number, answering it reluctantly. "Hi Toby."

"Hi, CC. How you doing?"

"I'm fine."

"I have some news about Lindsey. After we spoke, I made a couple calls. The police found an EpiPen in one of the maid's trash carts. She worked on the same floor where Lindsey was staying. The pen was intact, its seal was never broken. The police think she must have dropped it or lost it. The maid doesn't remember seeing it in any of the rooms, and no one reported missing one."

"That's interesting. I wondered why someone with such severe allergies wouldn't carry an EpiPen," CC said.

"I thought the same thing," Toby said. "Look, I'm coming to Chicago for a conference in a couple days. Could we have dinner? We could talk more about Lindsey."

CC rubbed her head, her migraine beginning. "I'm in Batavia now, and it's been pretty hectic. I've been away from the farm and the store. I'm really not sure I can get away."

Toby cleared his throat. "I understand."

CC could tell he was upset.

"We'll make it another time, CC. I have to go." He hung up.

"Who was that?" Anne asked, stepping out of the store, her arms loaded with bags of varying shapes and sizes.

"That was Toby."

"What did he want?" Anne sat next to her, holding her finger in front of her face, admiring her new sapphire and diamond filigree ring in the sunlight.

CC was momentarily distracted. "Anne, you weren't supposed to buy anything for yourself."

"It's not for me. I'm wearing it for safekeeping until I find someone on our list searching for a sapphire ring." Anne put her hand back down in her lap.

"Toby said that the police found an EpiPen in the maid's cart from Lindsey's floor. It was never used. They believe she dropped it."

"Seems like a lot of coincidences, doesn't it, CC? Lost EpiPens, lost scarves."

"Yes, it does. We better hurry. We're going to be late for dinner."

The early evening spring air was crisp and they could smell the lilacs their as they strolled the few blocks to Mrs. Eldridge's house. They could smell the pot pie wafting out of the English cottage. Mrs. Eldridge greeted them and sat them at the cozy dining table.

After her second helping, Anne sat back, letting her stomach expand, resisting the desire to undo the button on her jeans. "This was delicious," she said.

"It certainly was. Can you give me the recipe?" CC asked. "I'd love to share it with our fans on our blog."

"This would be wonderful at the Bee's Knees Café," Anne said.

"Excuse me?" Mrs. Eldridge said.

"In addition to the antique shop, we manage an organic bee farm with a small café."

"How delightful. I adore fresh honey."

"That's it. That's the ticket. We'll send you a case of honey for your recipe," CC said.

"Oh my goodness. Thank you." Mrs. Eldridge handed her the recipe, handwritten on an index card.

"Thank you, Mrs. Eldridge."

"Oh, dear, I asked you to call Alma."

"Yes, of course, Alma."

"How about a bit of mulberry wine to settle our stomach." She scurried out of the small dining room, returning shortly with crystal cordial glasses on a silver tray. She poured the deep red wine and passed them out. "Shall we toast, then? To Mary Todd Lincoln."

"Mary Todd Lincoln." Anne and CC repeated in harmony and drank the wine. Anne couldn't take her eyes off the bronze vase in the corner with the brightly colored gerbera daisy on it. "Is that a Heintz?" She had been watching a similar vase on eBay.

"Isn't it lovely?" Alma said.

Anne picked up the vase. It was symbolic of Heintz's Art Nouveau metal work, copper over bronze, four sterling silver flowers applied to its exterior. "This is lovely," Anne said, agreeing with Alma.

"That's one of my favorites. I have a whole room of vases, many of them left me by my mother and grandmother. Would you like to see them?"

Anne was out of her chair before she could answer. She followed Alma down the narrow hallway into a small bedroom. Wooden shelves lined the walls. Vases filled the shelves. Anne stood in the middle of the room, admiring the collection. There was Waterford crystal, Belleek porcelain, Chinese jade. Anne felt as if she was in heaven, her version of heaven. She picked up a matte green bottle vase, running her fingers along the tooled leaves. She had only read about these but never seen one in person. "This is a Grueby vase," she said, stuttering her words.

"Yes, dear. That belonged to my grandmother. It was a wedding present," Alma said.

"It's very special," Anne said. "Grueby pottery is hard to find, especially ones in this condition." She placed it carefully back on the shelf. Her eye was then drawn to a gray vase with leaves, stems and berries deeply incised in blue. Its interior was the same marine blue. "I've never seen one of these either. This is a Marblehead pottery vase from New England. Its color and shape make it very desirable for collectors. "

"That was also my grandmother's," Alma said.

"Alma, your collection is fantastic. Have you ever thought of parting with any of these?" Anne longed for the entire collection.

"Well, no dear, I haven't. Are they really that valuable?"

"Some of these are worth thousands of dollars."

"Well, I've always wanted to take my grandkids to Disney World. Could I really make that much?"

Anne smiled. " You definitely could." She coveted the blue Lalique parrots vase for herself, but knew she couldn't afford its $30,000 price tag, a conservative estimate at auction.

"Alma, do you think we could take a look at those journals?" CC asked.

"Of course, CC, where's my head? Let's go to the sitting room. I'll fetch them."

The room was cozy, with comfortable chairs. Anne sat next to CC on the flowered couch. She sank deep into the cushion. "Did you look at those vases?" Anne asked.

"I did. Let's stick to the journals for now. We can work out the vases later."

"Yes, yes, of course."

Alma returned, carrying a cardboard box. CC jumped up to help her. She set it on the coffee table. "You're welcome to look through it. There's a ledger and some notes. Some of these things really should be in the museum, but because they're my great-grandfather's I couldn't give them up."

CC carefully sorted through the papers. "This is interesting." She held up a book. Its cover read Patient Records. Opening it, she asked. "Who is this? I can't quite make out this name."

Alma placed her glasses on her nose. "That would be Dr. Horatio Kelly. He worked at the hospital at the same time as my great-grandfather. They were both there when Mary Todd was a patient."

CC turned to Anne. She read out loud. "Mrs. Lincoln's obsession with the dress continues. I've increased the laudanum to help with the headaches and to calm her nerves. She believes there is money hidden in the dress – millions of dollars. At her request, she had the patron bring her petticoat. She tore it open, revealing $10,000 inside it. Her fear of destitution has overwhelmed her. Her fight with the government to increase her widow's pension wages on. Each night she wakes up at 3 a.m. and strolls the halls, often disturbing the other patients with her wailing." CC flipped through the pages. "June 17, 1875. Mrs. Lincoln continues to write to her sister, Elizabeth, in Springfield, to take over her care. I've spoken to Robert Todd Lincoln, who shows great concern for his mother. It was his decision to have her committed to avoid a very probable tragedy. I have conferred with colleagues who believe her symptoms of insanity have their origins in some organic disease. She shows signs of anxiety and delusions. Her insomnia has contributed to these conditions. It has been ten years since President Lincoln's murder. More than enough reason to cause her distress. " CC flipped more pages. "Here's another entry. July 1. Attorneys James and Myra Bradwell have petitioned for Mrs. Lincoln's release. I am concerned about her obsession about the dress, blue with jet beading. In her deliria, she accused the staff of stealing the dress and her treasure. When we convinced her this was not the case, she wrote to the department of Civil War restitution to help locate an Isobel Grant. She believes Mrs. Grant has the dress."

"That's my dress," Anne interjected.

"Her delusions have gotten worse. She now walks the halls talking to herself about a treasure map sewn into the dress."

Anne's hand shook. She grasped the tiny cordial glass with

both hands.

"Anne, can I refill that for you?" Alma asked.

"Yes, please." Anne held out her glass.

As she filled it, Alma asked. "Anne, what is all this about the dress? I know that Mary Todd was obsessed about fashion. She spent thousands on dresses and had Elizabeth Keckley as her personal dresser, but what makes this dress so special?"

"She's talking about my dress. I have the blue dress."

"Are you sure it's the same dress?"

"She described it exactly. Jet beading, navy blue silk. It has Isobel Grant and Keckley's name sewn into it. There can be no other dress."

CC interrupted. "Anne, you've examined that dress with a magnifying glass. There's no map. There's no money," CC said before turning to Alma. "Are there any other mentions of Isobel Grant? We believe she was a slave who worked at Keckley's school for runaway slaves in Washington. That's all we've been able to find out."

"I've read the journals and patients' notes at least a thousand times, and that's the only mention of Isobel Grant," Alma said.

CC read from another entry. "Mrs. Lincoln returned quite agitated with a severe headache after attending a dinner party at the Picketts' house. After administering laudanum to calm her nerves, I performed hypnosis which I learned after studying the work of James Braid, the Scottish surgeon. His work with hypnotherapy proved to be quite valuable in helping soldiers from both sides after the war. While under hypnosis, Mrs. Lincoln stated Jonathan Pickett, the son of Thomas Pickett, came to Batavia in search of the dress. He confronted Mrs. Lincoln at the party about its whereabouts. Mrs. Lincoln's obsession even under hypnosis has caused me great concern for her sanity. I have found that women cannot handle their frail emotions. It is only through discipline and a strong hand that I can break through their hysterias. With other cases such as Mrs. Lincoln's, I have prescribed ice baths and restraints, but I am not allowed to prescribe such treatment on Mrs. Lincoln." CC stopped reading.

"This Dr. Kelly was a monster," Alma said.

"Unfortunately in that time, women were mistreated by mental health professionals. Look at Nellie Bly back in 1887. She went undercover at Blackwell's Island Insane Asylum. She wrote about the atrocities." CC recalled the story of the woman who inspired her to become a journalist.

"Yes, I understand the common practices at that time. Dr. Kelly did not follow them. I've read many notes on his other so-called treatments. It makes me sick to my stomach even to think about them," Alma said.

"What are you talking about?"

Alma flipped through the book and read, "Mrs. Alderwood's migraines and delusional dreams are caused by a brain infection. Women have weaker brains than men, leaving them vulnerable to such diseases. My experiments with similar cases lead me to believe these infections begin in the mouth. Bacteria enter the brain through the mouth, the portal of all germs. As a precaution for my other patients I've moved all their teeth."

"Ohmigosh, he pulled all her teeth?" Anne gasped.

Alma nodded her head and handed the journal back to CC.

"He mentions Jonathan Pickett. He was killed here in Batavia, wasn't he?" CC asked.

"Yes, an apparent home invasion," Alma said.

"Do we know any more about this Doctor Kelly?" CC asked.

"All I know is that Dr. Kelly was a surgeon during the Civil War. After the war, he treated soldiers for what we now call post-traumatic stress syndrome. He came to Batavia shortly after Mrs. Lincoln arrived here to provide treatment."

"Does he have any living relatives in Batavia?" Anne asked.

"The family left after Dr. Robert Kelly, Doctor Horatio Kelly's great-grandson, was committed in 1975. They didn't leave any forwarding information. I believe he had two daughters, twins. The house has been abandoned for years," Alma said.

Anne and CC stared at each other. "Committed? For what?"

"Schizophrenia and attempted suicide."

"Where is the house?"

"It's a farmhouse on the outskirts of town," Alma said.

CC thumbed through the last pages. "A lot of notes about daily exercise, walks in the garden. This is interesting. Mrs. Lincoln has been released to the care of her sister, Elizabeth, against my recommendations. She has arranged a trip to Virginia to visit the Pickett plantation, hoping to find the dress. I'm afraid I will not be able to cure her." CC looked up.

Shivering, Anne got up and peeked out the window. The grill of the VW bus smiled back at her. "The door's locked. It's safe," CC said.

"We better get back to the store."

They thanked Alma for dinner. Anne said, "Let us know if you want to sell any of your vases. We'll be glad to take them on consignment and even reduce our fee."

Alma hugged both girls and waved to them from her porch.

"You know, while we're here we should go check out the Kelly house," CC said as they got into the VW.

"We can't."

"Let's drive by and look. It's not that far." CC consulted the hand-drawn map that Alma had given her. Dusk was settling in, the country road was narrow. CC swerved into the ditch and corrected herself.

"Watch it," Anne said, glancing up from her watch list on eBay.

Slowing down, she drove by the old farmhouse, which was set back from the road. Gravel kicked up under the VW's tires. The front lawn was overgrown. There was nothing around for miles. "I could see why they wanted to leave," Anne said.

"Let's take a closer look," CC said, stopping the bus.

Anne jumped out, turned around, taking a last glance at the dress bag which was visible from the small window on the side of the bus. "Lock the bus."

"We won't be long. We're just taking a quick peek."

"Just lock the door."

CC obliged. A split rail fence wrapped around the house, but most of the rails had fallen and rotted. A small gate hanging half off its hinges swung with a sharp crack against the fence post. CC walked up the creaking stairs to the wraparound porch. The screen door rattled in the evening breeze. The porch windows were broken, screens torn.

Anne thought of Aunt Sybil's farmhouse on the North Shore of Chicago and the welcome she had received the day she had found her. This brought back unpleasant memories. "CC, let's get going. I don't like this."

CC opened the screen door, tapped on the front door which swung open. "It's not locked. No one has been here for a long time. Let's take a look inside." She took a flashlight out of her pocket. The front room was nearly empty except for a worn leather couch. The foil wallpaper peeled down the wall like someone was opening a Hershey bar.

"It smells moldy," Anne said, clutching CC's arm.

CC shined the light around the room, scaring away the mice and spiders who scurried to their safe spots. She started up the stairs.

"Come on, don't," Anne said.

"Anne, quiet." CC pushed open the first door in the long hallway.

"Remember that scene in *The Shining* with the twins at the end of the long hallway?" Anne shivered, the hairs on her arms standing upright.

"Don't be ridiculous."

The first three rooms were empty. They reached the last room, which was guarded by a heavy oak door. CC examined the heavy brass deadbolt on the hallway side. "Why would you have a deadbolt on the outside of a bedroom door?"

When she opened the door, it groaned with its weight. She shined her light in, revealing a large Victorian dollhouse dripping with cobwebs. In the corner of the room stood a small wardrobe displaying neatly hung doll dresses.

"This is really creepy." Several dolls stood at attention, garbed in Civil War-era dresses. One particular doll, a light-skinned African-American, wore a navy blue dress decorated with black beads. "I don't like this. Let's get out of here right now." Anne grabbed CC's shoulder again and tried to pull her back toward the door.

Behind them, the door slammed shut. Anne jumped with a shriek. CC dropped the flashlight. It spun like they were playing spin the bottle. As it spun, it lit up corners of the room. Glass doll eyes glowed back at them, bringing them to life.

"What's going on? " Anne screamed.

CC picked up the flashlight and then reached for the door-knob. She wiggled it, but it did not budge. "It's locked."

Anne ran to the window. There was no way to climb down. At least not without breaking a leg.

CC struggled with the door. They heard glass crashing and ran to the window. It was now pitch dark. CC's flashlight went dim and then out. Anne clutched CC's hand. "I left my phone in the car."

"Me too."

"What are we going to do?" Anne felt something slither over her foot, she screamed.

CC reached around in the darkness, trying to adjust her eyes. She walked along the walls, tapping on them.

"What are you doing?" Anne asked, clutching her arm.

"Trying to find a weakness in the wall," CC replied, continuing her tapping along the paneled walls. Thump. Thump. And then she heard a hollow reply. She pushed up against the wall. "Give me a hand, it's loose." They tugged until the paneling gave way. They could feel a breeze coming through the hole in the wall.

"What is this?" Anne asked.

"It must have taken hours for little hands to scoop away at this plaster," CC said, reaching in and pushing against the paneling on the other side. It popped off. They crawled through the tiny hole into the adjoining room. They carefully made their way downstairs as their eyes dilated, soaking up glimpses of the quarter moon coming through the broken windows.

They ran out of the house to the VW. The driver's window had been smashed, glass scattered along the ground and on the driver's seat.

Anne frantically searched the VW. "It's gone. The dress. It's gone."

Peril in Batavia, Spoon Sisters Blog

*D*EAR FRIENDS,

CC stopped. How much to tell? How much should they know? This blog was supposed to be about antiques, recipes and adventures in antique hunting, not murder mysteries. She continued typing.

I regret to inform you that my beloved VW was broken into, and Anne's dress was stolen. I will share more as we find out more.

CC stopped typing. Bandit stood guard facing the front door. He sensed her fear when she arrived home and never left her side. "Good boy, boo boo bear."

Anne went upstairs to her cozy apartment. The cats swirled around her feet, demanding attention. She fed them and put the teakettle on to boil. "The game's afoot," Anne said to the fuzzy gargoyles lined up in a row on the shelf over the kitchen table. Sassy plopped down and rubbed her head against Anne's arms. "I know, Sass. Aunt Sybil's teakettle. It's our thinking kettle, isn't it? How many mysteries have we pondered with this kettle on to boil?" As Anne waited for the tea, she made a fire and sat down in the leather wing back chair. Luna jumped onto her lap. "Luna, you're shedding all over my blouse. This is silk." Anne tried always to wear white or light colors because of Sassy and Sybil's shedding. She had given up trying to stay free of their cat hair. She stared down at the black hair against the snow-white blouse. A cat hair. She leapt up and ran to her purse and retrieved the plastic bag. She grabbed her phone and scrolled down her contacts to Sharon, her former colleague at Ebbort Labs. "Hi, it's Anne."

"Anne, I haven't heard from you in a while. It's so late. Is something wrong?"

"Sorry, forgot about the time. I have a huge favor to ask you. I have a sample I need a DNA test run on, actually two samples."

"Anne, I owe you, but security's been really tight lately."

"It's very important. It's a matter of life and death."

"I can't sneak you into the lab again."

"Can you run the test for me? It'll take too long if I send it out."

"I'll see what I can do."

"Thank you." Anne hung up as the teakettle screamed for attention. She settled back into her chair. She opened her first edition of Elizabeth Keckley's book. She had only had time to skim through it. She wouldn't sleep tonight anyway. It would be a good time to read it thoroughly. As she read, the Civil War began again. The white Persians versus the black cats. The truce had ended as the demand for her attention grew. Thankfully, after a few skirmishes, all four cats settled in around the fire and fell sound asleep. Anne could feel herself drifting, her eyes slowly closing again, jarring open. The gold ormolu clock on the mantle chimed, one, two, three times. It was 3 a.m., the hour Mrs. Lincoln wandered the halls of Bellevue Place like an apparition. She rubbed her eyes and began the final chapter. She read, "President Lincoln is intrigued by Isobel. I've seen them spend quiet hours conversing, tongues could wag over their intimacy, but that's not for me to say. Her owner has commissioned me to make a dress for his wife. Mrs. Lincoln is concerned about me traveling to the South, even with Isobel's master, Mr. Pickett, obtaining travel papers for us."

Anne's eyes drifted closed, and her hand on the book slipped, waking her. She continued reading. "Mrs. Pickett's emerald green dress was a great success. Several of her friends have requested dresses from me. Isobel was to return with me to Washington to continue teaching, but she was abducted by rebel soldiers. I tried stopping them, but they wouldn't listen. They honored my papers signed by Mrs. Lincoln and Mrs. Pickett. They accused Isobel of being a spy. She was terrified of damaging the gown I made her. Despite her pleas, they took her away before she could change.

The President himself commissioned me to make Isobel's dress. He said to help her travel between sides as a lady of means."

Dropping the book, Anne jumped out of her chair and grabbed her phone. "CC," she screamed when her friend answered.

"Anne, what time is it?"

"Isobel Grant was a spy. She was wearing my dress when she was captured."

"The dress is gone. You have to let it go," CC said.

"CC, there's something else. I was going to wait until the morning to tell you. I received a text from Sharon. You remember her? I used to work with her at Ebbort Labs." Anne didn't wait for an answer but continued, "She analyzed the cat hair I found on the hat I bought at Connie's store. The DNA matches Luna's. Connie lied to us. I think she was in Lindsey's hotel room. We have to confront her."

"Her sister's cat's hair isn't enough evidence to believe she was in the hotel room."

"Lindsey was missing a scarf. Every outfit had a matching scarf except the one she died in. Connie knew her sister wore matching scarves and was deathly allergic to latex. The cat hair we tested as a positive match to Luna's had traces of latex."

"I'll pick you up at 6 a.m.," CC replied, hanging up the phone.

Anne couldn't sleep, pacing back back and forth by the picture window inside Great-Aunt Sybil's Attic. The cats danced around her, vying for her attention except for Sassy, who would have none of it. She tolerated her daughter, Sybil's, nonsense but not these two strangers. She sat on a 1930s inlaid dry sink admiring her reflection in the polished copper tray. Anne walked over and caressed Sassy. "I know, girl, it's been a lot for you. We'll find a good home for both of them, I promise." Sassy neither purred nor hissed. Either would have been a recognition that the two black cats existed. She continued gazing at her reflection, lifting up a paw and cleaning it. "I love this dry sink, Sassy. I remember when I bought it from a dear friend who owned an antique store in Des Plaines, Fran King. Wonderful woman." Sassy meowed.

"Yes, you remember Fran, don't you? She always had a treat for you." Sassy crawled up Anne's arm. "I said treat, didn't I? Ok. Just time for a quick snack before I go. CC will be here before I know it. Ingrid is going to watch all of you while we take a short trip." Sassy sat back down. "It's not going to be that long. We'll be back late tonight." Sassy turned, wagging her tail ferociously and prancing away like a prima ballerina. Anne sighed and ran back to the front window.

The VW screeched out in front. CC waved from the driver's window, beckoning Anne. Ingrid walked into the store, and Anne hugged her young protégé. "Thank you for watching the cats."

"No problem, I have to open the store anyway. Dakota and her mom are coming by this afternoon."

"Give Sassy a little extra attention. She's been a little temperamental since our guests arrived."

"Of course. Anne, I'm so sorry about the dress. CC told me everything. Have the police been any help at all?"

"No, what can they do? The dress was there and then it's gone. Someone locked us in the house, broke into the bus, and left everything but the dress."

Ingrid shook her head. "Such a tragedy."

The horn honked again. Anne held up two fingers to CC through the store window. "Listen, Ingrid, if anything should happen, I want you to take care of the cats and take over the store."

"Anne, what are you talking about?"

"I'm just saying I want to make sure you're taken care of and the cats have a good home. And Dakota and her mom."

"I've never seen you like this."

"I don't feel good about this trip, Ingrid. This dress has been a curse from the day Isobel Grant put it on."

"Anne, don't go. You have me worried." Ingrid reached out her arm to pull Anne back.

Anne glanced over her shoulder at the picture of Great-Aunt Sybil hanging over the register. She knew she had no choice. It's what Great-Aunt Sybil would have done. She turned back and smiled at Ingrid. "I'm just being silly. It's been a long week. We'll call you when we get to Bloomington." Anne hugged Ingrid and kissed her cheek. Sassy leapt from the window and reached her paws up Anne's leg. Anne picked her up and cuddled her. Sassy purred ferociously. "Don't start, Sassy. If you're worried, I'm going to be worried. And please be nice to Luna and Reina. They're guests. You're in charge." Sassy sniffed Anne's face, taking a deep breath as if it might be her last of her beloved friend. Anne handed her over to Ingrid who walked over to the door, watching as Anne left.

CC rolled down her window. "Everything ok, Anne?"

"Yeah, sure, just giving some last minute instructions to Ingrid. Let's get going." Anne climbed into the VW, clutching her bag. Aunt Sybil had once told her when she was a little girl that everything you needed to survive you could fit in your bag. Reaching inside, Anne was comforted by the smooth silk of the Burberry scarf that had saved CC's life at the Cumberland Falls. She felt her jeweler's loupe, the key to discovering lost treasure.

"What's wrong?" CC asked, glancing at her friend.

"I've been thinking about the dress. Mary Todd believed it was a treasure map."

"I wouldn't trust Mary Todd's opinion. She suffered from mental illness," CC said. .

"Yes, I know, but she was obsessed with my dress. And she wasn't the only one. It seems that other people have been obsessed with it for over a hundred fifty years."

"You've gone over that dress with a fine-tooth comb. You've researched Isobel Grant and Elizabeth Keckley. There's no treasure map."

"Connie murdered her sister for that dress. They knew the stories of their great-grandfather and Mary Todd Lincoln's obsession with the dress. They made up their own Isobel Grant dress in their playroom. Schizophrenia runs in their family. That's a fifty-fifty chance that at least one of the twins was schizophrenic. Connie lied to us about Luna and Reina, and now we are going to confront her."

"Even if all the pieces of this puzzle add up, it's not enough for the police. Lindsey's death is still considered natural causes."

Anne was quiet. She wanted her one last perfect moment in case it was her last. That moment she would spend thinking of Nigel. The memory of staring into his eyes, feeling his bony arms wrap around her. She reached into her bag and felt the coolness of the steel against her fingers. She was neutral in the gun control battle. She carried it more out of respect for Nigel, who had given her the Lady Wesson .38 snub nose revolver. She never told CC because she knew she wouldn't allow it. If this were truly going to be their last adventure, Anne would not go quietly into the night.

"Are you ok?" CC glanced over.

Anne jerked her hand out of the bag as if CC could see through it. "Yes. How long until we get there?"

"About an hour. Why don't you close your eyes? You look very tired. "

" I'm fine." Anne turned and looked out the passenger window, taking in the cornfields and billboards. She thought, what an unpleasant last memory.

They arrived at Kelly's dress shop. The street was quiet, the sign on the front door was flipped to closed. CC called the number on the front of the building. From the other side of the door, they could hear a phone ring. CC tapped on the door; the phone kept ringing. She checked the doorknob. It twisted and the door opened. "Connie, are you here? Are you open?" she called out, walking along the aisles of clothes, Anne trailing behind her. She flipped on the light switch next to the front door. The crystal chandeliers glowed, illuminating the room and racks of dresses.

CC opened the changing room door. Anne walked behind the counter. She reached inside her bag, pulled out the gun, her heart pounding louder than her footsteps on the mahogany floors. She had felt the recoil of the Lady Wesson and knew what to expect. Nigel had made sure she was properly trained and had earned her Illinois concealed carry license. She didn't want to live in this world where she needed a gun, but that's the one she was in by circumstance and fate. She was an antique hunter and with that title came danger.

"Anne," CC screamed. "What are you doing? Where did you get that?"

"Nigel."

"Put it away. You're going to hurt someone," CC scolded.

She put the gun back in her purse. As she did, the gun went off, shooting a hole through the bottom of the bag—the large orange Prada bag. All her possessions scattered onto the floor.

"Are you ok?" CC rushed to her side.

Anne fell to her knees crying. "My bag." She cradled the large orange Prada bag, one of her most precious possessions. The bag had traveled everywhere with her, it was her lifeline. She couldn't lose it.

CC carefully lifted up the revolver with two fingers by the handle. She opened the cylinder and cleared out the rest of the bullets. "That's the last time you carry this."

"I'm sorry. I've just been so scared."

"Me too. I understand." CC knelt down and hugged her. "But there's nothing you and I can't get through together. We have each other, Annie, we have each other's backs, right?"

"Yes."

"Let's go. Connie must have stepped out for a while. We'll come back later."

"Ok, I'm just going to use the washroom." Anne gathered up her belongings, putting them into a plastic bag she grabbed from behind the counter. Her beloved purse would need surgery.

CC went to the front door. Sirens sounded in the distance. "Someone heard the gunshot." She yelled across the room. They would have to explain why they entered a closed shop and discharged a handgun. This would not go well. She was jarred from her thoughts when she heard the blood-curdling scream and turned around to see Anne standing in the open doorway of the bathroom. All CC could see were the dangling feet above Anne's head. She peered over Anne's shoulder to see the dead body of Connie Kelly wearing the blue Keckley dress. She stepped up next to Anne, put her arm around her shoulder. They both stared up into the lifeless eyes of Connie Kelly, hanging by a Hermes scarf.

Holding Cell, Spoon Sisters Blog

*D*EAR FRIENDS,
Lindsey Kelly's sister, Connie, is dead. An apparent suicide. Distraught from the passing of her sister and perhaps other notorious reasons to do with her sister's death, she is gone. Anne and I are being held for questioning as we found her. I've contacted a friend to expedite our detention.

She glanced up as the female police officer came up to her.

"Are you done, ma'am?"

She quickly typed.

Goodbye for now, toodooloo.

The policewoman took the laptop.

"Thank you so much," CC said.

The large woman of color knelt down and whispered, "I'm a big fan," and pulled a vintage cameo pendant out from under her uniform.

Anne adjusted her position. Her back ached from the hard steel bench in the holding cell. She jumped up as the female police officer escorted CC back. CC sat down next to Anne. "Don't you think we need a lawyer?" Anne asked.

"It's procedure. They let me call Toby."

"How's Toby going to help? Don't I get a call too?"

"Toby's working on getting us out. He knows the judge. He covered the police beat. He worked here before he moved to Springfield. The only thing they're charging us with is discharging a firearm."

"What about breaking and entering?"

"It wasn't breaking. The door wasn't locked, and it was during business hours."

"What about Connie?"

"Toby told me that Connie was on medication for schizophrenia and that she has a record of domestic violence. "

"Oh no, you think her husband?" Anne stopped.

"The domestic violence charge is actually against Connie. Her husband filed the police report," CC interrupted.

"Where is her husband?"

"They have him in for questioning."

"She hung herself, and she was wearing my dress."

"There's no information until the coroner's files his report and that won't happen until after the autopsy."

"Why would she put on the dress and hang herself? And why a scarf?"

CC shrugged her shoulders. Anne tapped her foot. "How long do we have to be in here?"

"They can't hold us for more than twenty-four hours unless they charge us. Either way, Toby made some phone calls."

"If Nigel were here, this would have been cleared up by now."

"Nigel's the one who trusted you with the gun."

"I have a license for it, CC."

"But not to discharge it in city limits. "

A guard came to the door, opened it, and said in a loud voice, "Hillstrom. Muller. You're free."

Anne resisted the urge to hug the guard. As they left the station, they saw Toby waiting for them. Anne checked her watch. It was almost 6 p.m. Surprisingly, she was starving.

"CC, your VW has been impounded," Toby said. "It's just paperwork. It'll be cleared up by tomorrow. Why don't I take you two out for dinner?"

"Sounds good." Anne jumped in the back seat of Toby's Honda. CC gave her a look and climbed in the passenger seat.

"Toby, thank you so much for coming to get us. I really just wanted you to make a couple phone calls. I didn't want to make you drive here."

"Not a problem. I called in some favors, plus how could I not help see for myself? A dead twin, actually two dead twins, a 150-year-old dress—it's something out of a crime novel."

"Welcome to our world," Anne piped in from the back seat as

she Googled Prada repair.

"With Connie's mental history, it appears to be suicide," Toby said.

"Two sisters dead in a matter of weeks. I think the police will look into it a little further," CC said. "What about her husband? He was kind of creepy."

"I didn't get any background on him. I'm sure I can talk to someone after the police are done interviewing him."

"I don't understand. You told me he filed domestic abuse charges against her, yet he was still working with her at the store."

"C'mon CC, you know the stories about domestic abuse. You must have covered this. People are either afraid to leave or feel they can make it better or change the other."

Anne piped up from the back seat, popping her head between the two seats. "Why the dress? Why was she wearing my dress? I'll never be able to put it on again."

"I spoke to the police psychologist. He believes Connie killed her sister and then herself."

"I knew it, I knew it, CC. Didn't I tell you? That's why she was wearing the dress. They both obsessed over the dress since they were little girls. And the scarf—that's why she hung herself with the scarf. Lindsey wore matching scarves with every outfit. It was Connie's way of admitting her guilt. She killed her sister over the dress, so she wore the dress to her own execution, and she hung herself with the murder weapon. Call the police and tell them to test the scarf for latex."

CC was quiet.

"Tell Toby about the hair—about Luna's fur."

CC didn't say anything.

"I found Lindsey's cat's hair on a hat I bought at Connie's store. Connie told us she hadn't seen her sister in years. And she didn't know anything about Lindsey's cats."

Not taking his eyes off the road, Toby reached under the driver's seat, pulled a manila file folder out, and handed it to CC. "What's this?" she asked.

"It's the police report on Lindsey Kelly. Check out the second page."

CC opened the file and read.

"What? What does it say?" Anne asked.

"Hang on." CC paused and then said. "They interviewed the front desk manager who was on duty when Lindsey died. She stopped at the front desk, saying she had forgotten her key."

"What time was that?" Anne asked.

"About the same time as our auction," CC said.

"Did they check the surveillance tapes? Was she wearing the Hermes scarf, the outfit she was wearing at the auction?"

"It doesn't mention anything about a scarf."

"It was Connie. Connie got the key. She rubbed latex on her sister's scarf. She knew she would change outfits. She had to know she would wear that scarf, and it would kill her," Anne said.

"I think she couldn't live with what she did," Toby said.

"Is there anything about seeing her leave?" Anne asked.

CC continued reading. "No, but she could have walked out undetected."

"How could you do that to anyone? Especially your own sister?" Anne asked.

"She was a very sick person. Abused as a child, on heavy medication for schizophrenia, in a volatile marriage," CC said. "All reasons to suspect her as the murderer."

"What do you mean suspect? She killed her sister," Anne said.

"It seems too perfect."

Anne was silent for a moment, letting CC's comment sink in. Her stomach growled. She remembered she hadn't eaten since breakfast. "Can we get something to eat and not talk about this? At least for the rest of the night." Anne reached into her bag and felt the fist size hole in the bottom.

"Toby, if you don't mind I think Anne's pretty shook up. Can you drop us at the nearest hotel?"

Toby put his hand on CC's leg and patted it gently. "Sure, I understand. You call me if you need anything."

CC slid a little closer to the passenger window, pulling her leg tight against the other. "We sure will. Thank you."

He stopped in front of the Bloomington Hampton Inn. Anne thanked him and leapt out of the car. They found a table at the restaurant. Anne perused the menu while CC made a phone call. She covered her mouth and spoke quietly. Anne peeked over the top of the menu and then resumed reading. The waitress came over. Anne ordered the Monte Cristo with fries extra crispy and a Diet Coke®. CC ordered the Nicoise salad. "Who'd you call?" Anne asked.

"I called Rachel."

"Why'd you call Rachel?"

"Anne, I was thinking about the passage you told me in Keckley's book. The night that Isobel Grant was taken by rebel soldiers."

"What about that?" Anne asked as the waitress put the plate in front of her. She took a bite of a hot, crispy fry.

"Both she and Keckley had letters of transport signed by both sides—Union and rebel. "

Anne took another bite. "And?"

"I was wondering why they took Isobel and let Keckley go. Isobel had papers from both Mrs. Lincoln and Thomas Pickett, a wealthy plantation owner in Virginia. Somebody knew she had a secret. I asked Rachel if she could get a list of the Virginia home guard. They were tasked with rooting out Northern sympathizers and spies. Anne, we have to follow the provenance of the dress. It's the only way we're going to find out who killed the Kelly sisters."

"You don't believe Connie killed herself and killed Lindsey?"

CC bit into her salad and said nothing.

After a restless night, the Spoon Sisters picked up the VW from the impound lot. They headed to Springfield to see Rachel, who had texted CC early that morning that she had some information, something that needed to be told in person. They met Rachel at the Supercup diner around the block from the Lincoln Museum. She was sitting in a back booth, sipping her coffee. She smiled when she recognized them. Anne and CC sat down across from her. "You two have been through a lot," she said.

"You have no idea," Anne said.

Rachel reached down on her seat and pulled up a notebook. She handed a piece of paper to CC. "This is a list of the Virginia home guard. At that time, it was composed of wounded soldiers, those too old or too young to fight on the front lines. I thought there'd be one name on there that you'd recognize."

CC scanned the list. "Dr. Horatio Kelly."

"No," Anne said, her eyes wide open.

"Yes, that same Kelly," Rachel said. "This is interesting." She pointed to a name toward the top of list. "This name here, Captain Richard Farmington, was wounded in the battle of Bull Run. He returned home to the town of Sidell, Virginia. It's a small hollow outside of Richmond where Thomas Pickett's plantation is. I did an ancestry search. His great-great-granddaughter's married name is Prima. "

Anne spilled her water glass, mopping it up with paper towels while listening.

"When they stopped Isobel, Pickett's slave, and found her carrying transit letters from both North and South, they realized she was delivering messages back and forth. When they confronted Pickett, they must have learned that he was a Northern sympathizer. They tortured and hung him. The rest of his family escaped," Rachel said.

"What happened to Isobel?"

"There's no mention of her because she was a slave," Rachel said.

"What about the dress? What happened to the dress?" Anne asked.

"Most likely due to the value of the dress, Farmington probably confiscated it for his wife," Rachel said.

"Pickett was a very wealthy man. If he was sending money to the North, he couldn't get it past Southern lines. He would have buried it, like much of the lost Civil War treasure," CC said. "Pickett must have given up the plan but not where the gold was buried. That's why his son went to Batavia to confront Mrs. Lincoln. She must have known about the plan to deliver gold to the Union. Dr. Kelly took a job at Bellevue Place to extract information from Mrs. Lincoln about the gold. When she told him about the dress, he must have realized that's where the secret lay, and if Mrs. Lincoln knew the secret, she wasn't telling. Kelly needed to bring her the dress. That's why he broke into Pickett's son's house looking for it, but Thomas Pickett Jr. didn't have it, so Kelly killed him. The only people who knew the secret were either now dead or crazy."

"I've been through the dress. There are no notes. There's no map. There's no gold in its seams. The jet beading is pretty but not that valuable at least by today's standards. Why the dress? Why a Keckley dress? Why an expensive dress?'

"Isobel was a house slave for Pickett. She was a nanny to his son." Rachel pulled out another piece of paper, which she showed Anne and CC. It was a picture of a tinplate. "That's Thomas Pickett, his wife Annabelle, their eldest son Thomas Jr. and their eight-year-old son Joshua."

CC stared into the poorly focused image. "Joshua's eyes are closed."

"Yes, he was blind since birth. Pickett commissioned a French tutor to teach him Braille."

"Rachel, thank you so much." CC jumped up and motioned for Anne to join her.

"Aren't we going to have breakfast?" Anne protested.

"No. Come on, Anne, we have to go." CC pulled her out of the booth seat. They left the restaurant and jumped into the VW.

"Hold on. I don't even have my seat belt on yet."

"The dress, we have to get the dress."

"It's still with the police."

CC fumbled for her purse, reaching behind her seat, swerving onto the road. She grabbed her phone. "Toby, it's CC. I need a big favor. How much clout do you have with the Bloomington Chief of Police? I need the dress, I will explain later, but I need the dress." She nodded her head, said goodbye, and threw the phone back at her purse.

"Slow down," Anne said. "What's this all about?"

"I don't want to say until we get the dress."

At 11:35 p.m. CC screeched to a stop in front of Great-Aunt Sybil's Attic. The only light on the entire block was from Buttersworth's Sweet Shop. Anne could hear laughter wafting through the window on top of the smell of caramel. "Rather late to be making sweets," Anne whispered. She unlocked the door, carefully balancing the dress bag. Ingrid greeted them, followed by a procession of black and white cats.

"So glad you're back, Anne," Ingrid hugged them both. "You two ok?"

"Yeah, everything's good."

"I've got class in the morning. If you two are good, I'm going to head home."

"Thanks, Ingrid."

Anne scooped up the cats. "I know, Sassy, I was gone longer than I thought." She carried them into the kitchenette and carefully placed the dress bag over a chair before giving them treats. She ran upstairs and grabbed her Doyle teakettle. Whatever CC was about to reveal, Anne felt she needed to have a part of Great-Aunt Sybil with her when she revealed it. She made a tea service and carried it to the dry sink in the storefront. She sat down on an overstuffed leather chair as she watched CC examining the dress she had draped over a dress form. CC circled the dress slowly, one finger on her chin thinking deep thoughts. She pulled out her iPhone. "What are you doing?"

"Looking something up. I need a pen and paper."

Anne ran to the cash counter, grabbed a receipt roll and pen. "Write this down for me." CC circled the dress, running her finger along the jet beading. CC called out letters, Anne wrote them down.

"Pickett," Anne said as she wrote the letters down. "What is this?"

"It's Braille. The treasure map is in Braille."

Anne took a sip of tea with a shaky hand. CC went back to the Braille alphabet open on her phone as she continued running her hand along each line of beading. By the time she was done, she was exhausted. She sank down into a chair next to Anne. Anne read out loud, "President Lincoln, Isobel is the mother of my child, so I trust her with my life. I believe as you do that this war must come to an end. With that in mind, I've buried a million dollars in gold to help you with that cause. I cannot transfer that much gold past the Rebel lines. It is buried in the outskirts of my plantation at these coordinates."

"Don't stop now." A voice rang out from behind them. Anne and CC jumped out of their chairs. Standing in the back doorway, Toby smiled. He shut and locked the door behind him. His white latex gloves glistened in the fluorescent lighting. "Toby," CC said.

"What? What are you doing here?" Anne asked.

"CC, I have to say I'm pretty disappointed in you. I rather admired you as a journalist. I put the pieces together a while ago."

"All those interviews at the Lincoln Museum. All those stories. You were very helpful weren't you?" CC asked.

"Lindsey was an attractive woman. It started as a fascination. The more I learned about the dress and her sister, it became something else."

"Then you saw my blog about the dress."

"I said I always admired you. I've been following your blog and your charming stories about the famous Spoon Sisters, the journalist, the chemist, the crime fighters."

Anne reached for her phone.

"I've already killed two sisters. Don't think I won't kill two more."

Anne put her hand in her lap.

"Sit down." Toby pulled up a chair and sat across from them. They could see the outline of the gun in his waistband. He reached in his coat pocket, pulled out a packet of cigarettes, and lit one.

"You can't smoke in here," Anne said.

"Really, Anne?" CC whispered. "Toby, we were close at one time. I have to believe you still feel something for me."

Toby laughed. "You broke my heart, CC." He puffed his cigarette.

"I'm sorry, Toby, I didn't mean to," CC whispered. "You've had a good life. You're a successful editor; you have the bar."

Toby flicked his cigarette to the floor, stamping it out. He thought for a second and then picked it up. "No reason to leave evidence now. Editor of a small Midwest paper. And the bar," he laughed. "The bar has never made money. Another month, it'll be closed."

"Why kill Connie?" CC asked.

"She was waiting in Lindsey's room when I got there. At first, I thought it was Lindsey. I couldn't tell them apart either. She came for the dress. Lindsey contacted her and told her about it. Even though they hated each other, she couldn't help but share that moment with her sister. I convinced Connie to let me get the dress from Lindsey. She never asked how. I don't think she cared—she was obsessed. Their deranged father spent his life searching for the dress, and he passed that obsession on to them. At first I thought that's all it was—an obsession of two delusional sisters. Until Lindsey showed me her great-grandfather's personal journal, the one he kept separate from his patient notes. Under hypnosis Mrs. Lincoln told Dr. Kelly the whole plan, Pickett's buried gold, a lost treasure map, but she left out the Braille sewn into the dress. That was genius."

"And Connie figured out you killed her sister, so you had to kill her," CC said.

Sassy leapt onto Anne's lap. Anne was shaking. Sassy hissed at Toby. "When you called me to help you get the dress back from the police, I knew you found the secret. The famous Spoon Sisters couldn't let a mystery stay unsolved. I'll take the coordinates of the gold now." He held out his hand.

Anne started handing him the paper, and then she shoved it in her mouth and ate it.

Toby jumped up to grab her. Sassy jumped on him, clawing at his face. Sybil came out of the shadows and jumped on his back. Luna and Reina ran between his legs, tripping him. Anne took the teapot and bashed him over the head, knocking him out cold, leaving a large dent in the teapot and one in his head. Anne grabbed several scarves and tied him up tight while CC called the police.

The entire street in front of the antique store was lit up with Glen Ellyn squad car lights. Betsy Buttersworth watched from the sidewalk along with the crowd of reporters. Anne and CC took turns telling the entire story to the police detective.

Nick pulled up and ran over to CC, hugging her and lifting her off the ground. He looked her over. "Are you ok?"

"Fine, I'm fine."

He kissed her. "I love you, marry me."

"What?"

"Marry me."

CC just smiled.

"I, I wanted to propose over a candlelight dinner, a little more romantic then standing in the middle of the street surrounded by cops. It just came out of me."

"No, it's very romantic. I love you too." CC cupped his face in her hands and kissed him.

"Don't give me an answer right now, I want to do it right. We'll talk later. You look exhausted, get some sleep."

As the sun came up, the street cleared. Anne and CC went up to Anne's kitchen and sat down at the table, sipping tea. All four cats lined up on the shelf above them. Anne glanced up. "That's funny."

"What?"

"Reina's sitting next to Sybil, and Luna's sitting next to Sassy. This is the first time I've ever seen them do that."

CC reached up and scratched Luna's head. "Thank you, girl." CC texted.

"Who are you texting?"

CC held up her finger. "Just a second." She raised her phone and took a picture of the cats and started typing again. Her phone pinged. "That was Rachel. She would love to adopt Reina and Luna."

Anne clapped her hands. "That's wonderful."

CC yawned. "I'm too tired to tell her everything. I'll call her after I get some sleep."

"What about the gold? Do you think it's really there? Will we get a reward?"

"The detective said he contacted the Virginia police. They are sending a crew out there to dig. The plantation is owned by the state."

Anne nodded. CC yawned again.

"Why don't you go lie down in my bed? I'll sleep on the couch."

"Are you sure?"

"Yes, I'll be fine."

CC walked over and kissed Anne on the forehead. "I love you, Sis."

"I love you, too." Anne went into the hall closet, grabbed a down comforter and pillow, and sank down onto the couch. Sassy jumped up and stretched across the back of the couch. Anne reached for her phone to check the time—7:30 a.m. She yawned and snuggled into the arm of the couch. "Goodnight, Sassy." As she was about to drift off, her phone rang. She startled awake and grabbed it. "Hello, who is this?"

"Annie, it's Nigel."

Anne sat upright on the couch. "Nigel, I have so much to tell you."

"Anne, come tell me in person. They said I could see you."

Anne counted to ten, moving her lips. "Nigel, no more of this nonsense. You tell me right now what you've been up to, otherwise I'm hanging up and never speaking with you again."

"Anne, my uncle died."

"Nigel, I'm so sorry. Why didn't you tell me?"

"I haven't seen him since I was a little boy. He disowned my mother when she married my father."

"Why would he do that?"

"Because my father wasn't a royal. My uncle was the Earl of Stanwick. When he died, I inherited his castle and all his lands."

Anne burst out laughing. "You want me to come to your castle?"

"Anne, I'm serious here. Yes, I want you to be come to my castle, and I want you to be Lady Anne Towers."

While Anne dreamed of castles and tiaras, CC opened her laptop.

Final Thoughts, Spoon Sisters Blog

*D*EAR FRIENDS,
I promised that as the mystery unraveled, I would keep you up to date. There is so much to tell you, but I'm exhausted. I feel like you've been with me on this entire journey, so I felt it only right to include you at the journey's end. I promise to write you in the morning. Until then, dear friends, toodooloo.

As she started to close the browser, she noticed a new comment from Dr. Smart. "I hope in some small way that I was of service to you and that you will depend on my expertise in the future."

CC's Recipe

HAM PALACSINTA

Hungarian pancake batter (similar to French crepes)
1 cup flour
pinch of salt
4 eggs
1 cup milk
3 tablespoons butter

Combine flour, salt, eggs and milk until smooth. Chill one hour. Heat crepe pan, coat with oil, ladle batter on pan and tilt to cover pan. After first side is cooked, cook on second side. Use parchment paper to layer crepes between sides.

FILLING

½ pound ground cooked ham
½ cup sour cream
Mix ham and sour cream together.

Layer small amount in crepe and roll and tuck corners.

Beat two eggs.

Cover crepes with flour, then dip in egg mixture then in bread-crumbs. Place in pan with hot oil. Fry slowly until golden brown.

Serve with honey mustard to taste.

About the Author

Vicki Vass gave up her reporter's notebook to chronicle the near real-life adventures of her two best friends and fellow Antique Hunters. Like the fictional Anne, Vicki enjoys shopping and is always on the hunt for the next great deal. The first book in the series, *Murder for Sale,* was a finalist in the Mystery & Mayhem contest.

Most recently, she published *Bloodline,* the first book in the Witch Cat Mystery series and *Gem Hunter* based on her real-life quest for precious stones. When not writing, Vicki can be found walking her two Australian shepherd puppies, Atticus and Tracker.

Books by Vicki Vass

ANTIQUE HUNTERS MYSTERY
Murder for Sale
Pickin' Murder
Killer Finds
Key to a Murder

Bloodline: A Witch Cat Mystery, book one

Gem Hunter: An Alex Kustodia Mystery

The Postman is Late: A Neighborhood Watch Mystery